I0691378

Obsessions

First Edition

Published by The Nazca Plains Corporation
Las Vegas, Nevada
2009

ISBN: 978-1-935509-44-8

Published by

The Nazca Plains Corporation ®
4640 Paradise Rd, Suite 141
Las Vegas NV 89109-8000

PUBLISHER'S NOTE
Obsessions is a work of fiction created wholly by *Christopher Trevor*'s imagination. All characters are fictional and any resemblance to any persons living or deceased is purely by accident. No portion of this book reflects any real person or events.

Cover Photo, Anetta
Art Director, Blake Stephens

DEDICATION

To Scott J.

In my days as a banker you were MY obsession...

Obsessions

First Edition

Edited by
Christopher Trevor

CONTENTS

INTRODUCTION

Obsessions, what are they really? Sometimes obsessions are things, persons and thoughts that we cannot live without, or perhaps one may have convinced one's self that they cannot live without whatever their obsession is. Some would say that an obsession is a compulsive preoccupation with a fixed idea or perhaps an unwanted feeling or emotion, often accompanied by symptoms of anxiety. An obsession could also be an unreasonable idea that one cannot divorce themselves from. I see this as Obsessions and Obsessive Compulsive Disorders going hand in hand. Those of us obsessed with feet (as I have been known to be) would look at this as going foot in hand I suppose. An obsession is also defined as something that preoccupies a person to the exclusion of other things. Psychiatry defines obsession as a persistent idea or impulse, often associated with anxiety or mental illness.

Obsession can also be defined as an irrational motive for performing trivial or repetitive actions, sometimes even against one's will, again, I think of Obsessive Compulsive Disorder here.

In this latest collection of author's erotic tales (and one of my own) I have pooled together a group of writers that I asked to write an erotic story about what obsesses them the most. Those who know me, those who have read my work, and those who have met me know that my own obsessions are all related to male feet, predominantly black socked male feet and all the twisted and evil connotations that one can think of to do those black socked male feet. In the story that I contributed to this collection of obsessive tales starring my soon to be recurring character "Greg Smith", a handsome and hunky executive winds up stripped down from his business suit to what some would call his black office socks and he finds himself bound up in a most heinous yet mortifying position. In this tale my obsessions range from business attire, black socked feet and bondage, all things that seem to rule my world. When it comes to business attire Greg Smith is, (at least I think so) one of my greatest fictional characters (and yes, he is an obsession) ever created. Greg defines the well-dressed man.

Quote from Greg Smith himself concerning business attire and accessories: *"The right suit, properly tailored, or even custom made for a man radiates the confidence of the man who wears it. Some men call their business attire their power suits, yes, power, yet they maintain an air of masculine dignity when attired in that suit of power. The proper white shirt and silk (make sure its real and pure silk) power tie emanates that a high-powered executive knows the importance of a clean cut and proper appearance. Lastly, the OTC (over the calf) dark colored dress socks and his highly shined lace-up shoes complete what I refer to as the "Executive Package." It's my obsession and Christopher Trevor writes about it very well in his erotic fiction."*

But besides my own obsessions this time out I offer you other author's obsessions.

Newest author to my fold is Logan Zachary, writer of the story that leads this book off, "Corner Office." Mr. Zachary wrote "Corner Office" for several reasons and he states: *"I wrote the story "Corner Office" for several reasons. First, and the most important reason being that the Grand Master of fetishes, Christopher Trevor" asked me to write a story for this latest publication. I submitted some of my writing to Mr. Trevor over time and he has offered me some of the kindest and most insightful opinions on my work that any author could ever ask for. I am humbled and honored by the time he has taken to make my writing even better. With "Corner Office" Christopher liked what I wrote and said that it fed some of his own obsessions where businessmen and their attire are concerned. Also, I wrote this story because the voyeur in all of us needs to be fed and addressed. How many times have we driven past an open window and just happened to see a nude vision of perfection, well-muscled, hairy and hard? Do we go around the block, stop traffic and knock on the door? Well, that is mostly up to the individual. The last reason I wrote this story is, that like Christopher Trevor I enjoy seeing a handsome man in a suit having sex in the workplace. This plays on the forbidden, the total taboo yet totally erotic and daring. In "Corner Office" I have fed the fantasy about the person beyond the open window who is hot, hairy and hard. Then, I put a business suit on him that fit his well-muscled body just right and I like to think you have the makings of a hot scene, an obsession if you would. It shines a good light on the words "Big Business."*

Needless to say I was very flattered that Mr. Zachary referred to me as the "Grand Master" and that he employed some of my own fetishes and obsessions in his hot and scorching tale, "Corner Office."

Returning author Nicholas Bowman has this time out offered us a sequel to his story "The Music Lesson", which appeared in my book "Discipline", entitled, "The Basic Lesson." I have found that corporal punishment and music are two of Mr. Bowman's obsessions as once again a street musician finds himself, and his rear at the end of a belt. Mr. Bowman truly mixes two of his fetishes well in this tale of corporal punishment and music.

Another returning author, Anonymous Cop joined me in writing the tale "The Cop and the Jogger or The Jogger and The Cop." (To be truthful this story was written more by Anonymous Cop than me.) One of Anonymous Cops' obsessions is the capture and humiliation of unsuspecting police officers, as was found in my book "Blackmail" with his stories "No Choice" and "This Little Piggy." I can attest to a fetish for writing in this subject matter as well, seeing as some of my stories in the past have revolved around and starred captured cops. The story "The Cop and the Jogger or The Jogger and the Cop" truly captures (pun intended) a man's twisted and diabolical obsession when he ruthlessly and stealthily captures a handsome cop and wreaks his own brand of vengeance on the hapless and unwitting officer.

Justin Tyler, whom I dedicated my book "Humiliation" to, shares some of my obsessions when it comes to black socks and male feet. In this book Mr. Tyler shares his writing talent and another of his obsessions in the story "You're Fired!" Mr. Tyler enjoys creating fiction where a dapper, well dressed man is slowly, methodically, forcefully and rudely stripped of his garments that make up his manly and elegant appearance. In "You're Fired" all of this comes together and is stripped away beautifully and originally. Mixing his fetishes with a thirst for revenge Mr. Tyler has proven his writing prowess.

The book is rounded out with the story "Photo Shoot." Those who have read Ron Bossman's stories in the past know his obsessions with erotic looking underwear and bondage. In this story penned from an actual experience/photo shoot Mr. Bossman shows us his obsessions for voyeurism, exhibitionism, bondage, photography and hot looking underwear.

I thank all the authors of this latest book for their time, their creativity and their friendship.

Happy Reading.

- Christopher Trevor-

CORNER OFFICE

Written by Logan Zachary

Wrapping the fluffy towel around my waist, I wiped the steam from the mirror. My reflection looked back at me and asked, "What are your strengths and weaknesses?"

I rubbed the bulge beneath the towel.

"This is my strength, and hot sexy men are my main weakness," I whispered.

My bare feet slapped across the tile floor and I walked toward the bed. The view from the window was breathtaking, the New York City skyline, tall buildings and lights.

My briefcase rested by the television. I wanted to review the company's information one more time, but the scene in front of me pulled me to the glass. The cool surface refreshed me from my shower, my body still damp in the towel.

The sixtieth floor view filled this Midwest farm boy's eyes. Trees and Minnesota lakes held nature's beauty, while these showcased man's architectural abilities.

Rows and rows of cars streamed along the tunnels of roads. Reds moving away, white coming forward. Dots ran across the street as the lights changed. The city never slept, and I doubted that I would.

This hotel room sat in the corner overlooking a busy intersection. Three other buildings stared back at each other. Lights burned in some windows, while others were a patchwork quilt of color, shade and light.

My interview was at ten the next morning across the street. My eyes peered at it and wondered where I would be working? Will they hire me? Was this trip in vain? My mother said to always think positive, so I nodded to my faint reflection. I will get this job. My gaze played along the building and stopped. A corner office blazed with light. The blinds were pulled back, revealing an easy view of the man sitting at his desk.

The black haired man had thick waves that covered his head. He typed frantically on the computer keyboard, sipping from a mug on his desk. His suit coat lay across the back of his desk chair and his tie was over that. He ran his fingers through the curls and they sprang back into place.

I pressed my body against the window, the cold descended on my flesh, refreshing me, but a stirring occurred beneath the towel. I looked down to see if anyone could see up my towel, and laughed at my sixtieth floor height.

The man swiveled his chair around, his back to the desk. His white shirt was open a few buttons, a thick mat of black fur stuck out of the "V".

I pressed myself harder against the glass. A small mist of vapor escaped from my mouth and condensed on the glass. I tried not to breathe so I wouldn't fog my view.

The man leaned back in his seat and closed his eyes. One of his hands rested on his chest. His fingers touched the pelt on his chest. Mindlessly, they combed through the mass and seemed to savor his touch. His hand slid down his shirt and opened another button. His other one played across his lap and stroked slowly, up and down along the zipper. His tight fitting dress slacks hugged his body at every curve as the bulge grew in his crotch.

Another button opened and a row of well-defined abs peeked out from under the fur. His finger traced down the middle furrow.

My cock swelled and pulled my towel loose from around my waist. The cotton slipped from my hips and I tried to catch it, but my hands weren't fast enough. The towel circled around my ankles and my cock slapped the window. The cold sent a shockwave through my skin and seemed to fire up my spine and burn into my brain. I bent and grabbed the bath towel and held it in front of my pelvis.

The man stared up at me. My whole body jolted from the realization.

He nodded and smiled. His finger pointed to my towel.

I pressed it against me tighter and looked around in the other windows, seeing if anyone else had seen. No one else appeared to be looking at me. Then I realized how much of me was still exposed. My bubble butt was firm and round and I felt it could be seen from various angles in this corner window. I wrapped the towel around my waist and fastened it tighter.

The businessman shook his head.

It was my turn to point at him. I motioned as if I were unzipping his pants and wiggled my finger at him.

He pointed down at his torso. He unbuttoned the last two buttons on his dress shirt and pulled it wide open. His perfect torso, abs, and hair made my mouth water. A thick treasure trail disappeared into his pants.

I nodded and smiled. My finger made the unzipping motion again.

Mr. Suit unbuckled his thin belt and slowly unhooked the clasp. He pinched the zipper tab and pulled it down, inch by slow inch. White cotton briefs came into view. The waistband looked like Calvin Klein's to me. There was a huge bulge in the open "V" of his pants. He pointed down.

I nodded and signaled to pull down his pants.

He grabbed the flaps and made circles with them. He pulled them wide and low and back up to cover himself.

He was such a tease, and my body was responding.

He raised his butt in his chair and spilled his slacks down. His hairy knees came into view. His legs were muscular and well defined. They were evenly covered with hair, and a deep, rich tan, just like his chest.

His white briefs contrasted nicely with his skin, his healthy, sun-kissed skin.

My body started to sweat, despite the cold glass.

Mr. Suit motioned to my towel.

I gave him the "No-No" with my hand, but pointed back to his lap.

He combed down his chest and worked his way down to his underwear. His fingers played along the elastic waistband and slipped a finger underneath. He slipped another finger in from his other hand and pulled them down. His pubic bush burst out from under his briefs. A flash of flesh peeked out and he replaced them. He rubbed himself and worked down his leg. He slipped a finger in and pulled the leg hole open.

More hair poured out, as a tan line was seen.

I licked my lips and cupped my hands to the window, focusing my attention on what he was showing.

He motioned back to my towel.

I reached down and pulled up one corner, revealing a leg. It slipped out from between the folds. I pointed my toe and showed my athletic leg in all its glory. Running five miles a day kept me toned and tight.

He nodded in agreement, as he worked under a leg hole. He slipped his hand inside and fondled himself. He pulled the leg hole wide and a testicle fell out. The furry ball rested against his leg and bounced on his chair. He pulled up on his briefs and it rose and dropped. It was heavy and low dangling, well hung. He reached inside and pulled on the other one. The orb peeked out and dropped back in. He pulled on the cotton and both balls were exposed.

My cock jumped and strained against the towel, now held firmly against the window, which was no longer cold, but warmer, moving to hot.

He waved at me and turned his hand palm-up, saying, "Your turn."

I moved my leg to the side, widening my stance. Spreading them wider, my hand pulled the towel up and a cool breeze swirled around my leg and ran over my balls. The hair fluttered in the air. The opening of the towel widened, and my balls swung free. I rocked my hips and made them pendulum back and forth.

Mr. Suit's pelvic thrusts made his pair swing in time with mine. He ran his hand along his Calvin's, outlining his erection and milked it. A wet spot was forming at the tip in the cotton. He pulled his length to the side to keep that length covered. He then pulled the top of his underwear down and revealed his thick triangle and part of a meaty shaft. It was thick and veined, white against the black hair and deep tan. He kicked off his shoes and kicked his legs to free them from his gray slacks. The weight of his wallet and keys helped pull them off his legs. Black knit socks covered his feet.

He spread his legs wider and both balls were hanging free down one underwear leg hole. He worked his erection under the briefs and stretched them.

I strained to see more details of his cock.

He shifted his cock and pulled the waistband down, down to its base. The thick shaft hid under the cotton as he pulled his balls out and let them hang out. The weight of his testicles pulled the shaft and the fat tip slipped out from under the waistband. The tip painted a wet streak across his hairy belly.

I pressed my pelvis against the window and let the towel open. My left leg was completely exposed and my penis held the towel in front of me.

Mr. Suit pulled his shirt off and let it flutter to the floor. He spun his chair around to face the desk and pulled open a drawer.

"Don't turn away now," I said.

As if he heard me, he spun back to face me. He proudly pulled his underwear off and let them slide down his legs. His socks covered feet kicked them off. His beautiful erection stood straight up from his perfect hairy body. He picked up a small bottle and squeezed out a palm of lotion. He smeared it down his shaft and jacked the raging hard-on.

I pressed my cock against the window and humped it. Pre-cum oozed out with each push and slid down my dick.

Mr. Suit's head fell back as he jacked off. A smile played across his face as he enjoyed his body and the work of his hand. He extended his legs and spread them wide.

I couldn't believe what I was seeing. My body tingled all over. Backing away from the window, the towel fell to the floor.

Mr. Suit stopped and stared. He slowly stood up and licked his lips.

I stroked myself and pressed my erection against the window. The pre-cum made my dick slide across the glass smooth and easy. I backed and jacked, then pressed against the window, humped for several strokes and then I backed and jacked again.

Mr. Suit followed my lead. He stepped up to the glass and rubbed his dick up and down. He stepped back and whipped his penis hard. He set his legs wide apart and arched his back. He worked his hand faster and faster on his aroused flesh. His balls pulled up alongside of his shaft as he worked his meat. He stroked faster and faster. I followed him stroke for stroke. My balls tightened too. The pressure grew and grew filling my body, starting in my toes and running up my legs and along my spine.

An eruption followed from my balls through my pelvis and down along my shaft. I pressed my cock against the window, hoping the cool would slow the pleasure, but the new stimuli made my cock explode across the glass.

Mr. Suit watched as I frosted the glass. His pounding pushed him to the window, the wet outline of his cock moved up and down, and a huge thick load shot out of his tip and sprayed out in a perfect fan of cum. He humped the glass, smearing his balls to the window and spread his seed.

Cum dripped down the window and along my cock. The thick cream seeped through my hair and flowed over my balls. A long rope of cum stretched from them and slowly made its way to the floor.

Mr. Suit stepped back from the window and drew a smiley face in his cum. He smiled, blew me a kiss and flipped the vertical blinds closed, ending my view of perfection.

My legs collapsed and I sat down hard on the floor. My ass bounced off the thick carpet. I lay back on the floor and stared at the ceiling as my heart rate returned to normal.

Guess I needed to hit the shower again.

The phone rang, it was my courtesy wake up call, and woke me from my dreams. My morning wood stood up straight and proud. The soft sheets felt great against my aroused flesh. My cock, still tender from last night's workout, wanted more. I jacked off quickly, as I replayed last night in my mind.

The rest of the morning flew by, a shower, a quick breakfast, and I was dressed and ready for my interview. I walked across the street to the building of my voyeur stud of last night.

Before I left I looked over to his window, but the blinds remained closed and no signs of life occurred. As I neared the front door my heart quickened, me thinking that maybe I'd run into him in the lobby, in the elevator, in the bathroom...

But what did he look like? I couldn't remember his face. Did I even look at his face?

"Sean Robinson?" the secretary asked.

I nodded and covered my groin with my attaché case, afraid my pants revealed my aroused state.

"Here is your schedule for the interview today," she said and handed me a folder with the Sloan and Associates logo on the cover, embossed in gold.

I flipped open the folder and looked at the timeline.

    10:00 - Human Resources and Benefits

    10:30 - Chris Knight (Divisions and Departments)

    11:00 - T J Sloan (Owner and Developer)

    12:00 - Lunch

    1:00 - Wrap up and Questions

"I hope that makes sense to you," the blonde said, waiting for a reply.

"Looks like a full morning," I replied with a smile.

"If you take a seat over there, Chris Knight will be with you shortly to take you on a tour and get you to Human Resources."

"Thanks," I said and took a seat.

The morning sped by, and I heard about benefits and salary scales. I toured the different floors of the company and saw everything, from the bottom to the top.

Chris Knight finished our tour and took me to the final interview.

"I hope all your questions have been answered," he said and knocked on the door that he had led me to and waited for a response.

"Come in," a voice called from inside.

Chris opened the door and pushed it open.

"I have another meeting I need to be at, so I'll leave you here with Mr. Sloan," Chris said and extended his hand and shook mine.

"Thanks so much," I said.

"I hope you'll be joining the family soon," Chris said, released my hand and left.

I looked into the office and saw a man sitting behind a big desk. He spoke into the phone and held up his hand, welcoming me in. He pointed to the chair opposite his desk.

I entered slowly and inhaled. The smell of home greeted me.

Mr. Sloan set the phone down and stood up. He was a handsome man of forty years. His black hair was slicked back, and a neatly trimmed mustache covered his upper lip. His tailored suit fit him like a glove. His shirt was white with a midnight blue tie. I walked to his desk and took his hand. It fit mine perfectly.

"Mr. Robinson, welcome to Sloan and Associates," Mr. Sloan said.

"Thank you Mr. Sloan," I replied. "Thanks for choosing me for this opportunity."

"Well, we look for the right person for each of our positions," he said. "And I feel that you would fit in here."

Before I could say anything the intercom beeped.

"Mr. Sloan, the messenger has arrived with that contract that needs to be signed before noon," the voice on the intercom said.

I looked around the corner office and felt I had seen it before.

Mr. Sloan stood up and bowed slightly.

"I'm sorry for this, but I need to attend to this matter," he said.

I stood and said, "I understand. Take your time, I'll be here."

Mr. Sloan walked around his desk and left the room. His suit whispered with each step.

I walked over to the wall and saw diplomas, awards, pictures and magazine covers with Mr. Sloan's picture on them. The blinds behind his desk were closed, but the ones opposite were open. I moved over to enjoy the view. It looked like the view from my hotel room window.

I turned to the closed blinds. Could it be? Right here in front of my face?

Mr. Sloan was gone. The desk looked like the one, and so did the chair.

There was only one way to find out, and this was my chance. I slipped around his desk and pushed the chair over. I snuck over to the blinds and pulled the hanging slants back. A wet, sticky outline of a cock marred the otherwise immaculate window. A thick white, creamy fluid ran down the pane and a smiley face grinned back at me.

Instinctively, I reached forward and touched a rivulet. It was still wet.

I rolled the liquid between my thumb and index finger, as I slowly brought it to my nose. Inhaling deeply, a musky man scent assaulted my nostrils, sweat and sex. My tongue desired a taste of the salty, sweet cream.

A hand touched my shoulder, and I whirled around.

"I enjoyed our show last night, I'm still hard you see," Mr. Sloan said, grabbed my hand and held it to his fly.

I could feel the massive erection. It was thick, hot and throbbing.

"You? Did you? Was I...?" I stammered, my mind whirling in so many directions.

Mr. Sloan smiled. His wonderful, kissable lips lit up his handsome face. He leaned forward. I titled my head. Last night flooded my mind with naked images and my heart rate increased making me swell and grow in my suit trousers.

"Mr. Sloan..." I started as his lips brushed mine.

"TJ," he whispered into my mouth, and then our lips met. "Call me TJ."

Heat radiated through my body, making my cock grow to full length.

He stepped closer. His body pressed against mine.

I could feel his arousal as it rolled against mine, suit pants to suit pants. Our mouths opened as the kiss intensified. As the kiss deepened our tongues met and my knees went weak. I wrapped my arms around his muscular torso and pulled him tight. My pelvis ground into his. Mr. Sloan pulled back and loosened his tie. A tuft of chest hair peeked out of the top of his shirt.

My finger reached forward and touched it. I pressed deeper and felt the warmth of his skin. Digging in deeper, the coarse hair tickled my finger, and I wanted more. I wanted to run my whole hand over his chest, through his furry chest hair and down to the thick bush and lower.

"Let me lock the door," TJ said.

I didn't know what to do. Last night it was a fantasy. It had been a jack-off session in front of a window that felt great, but this was different. This was real.

TJ stood by and waited.

"We don't..." I began.

I reached forward and took his hand. His warm touch ignited me. My whole body relaxed under his hands. I unbuttoned his shirt and combed through his chest hair.

TJ took my caress as an invitation. He loosened my tie and started to unbutton my shirt. His hand reached inside my shirt and explored what he had seen last night.

"It feels even better than it looked last night, and I can't wait to see how you taste," he said to me.

His tongue traced my lips and sought entry.

I pulled his shirt out of his suit pants and undid the last button. The view of his torso and the perfect pelt made my mouth water. My fingers combed through the soft hair. My tips rode the crests of the pecs, slipped down the valley between, and roller-coastered over his six-pack. I explored his bellybutton, which funneled his hair into a vortex. The scent of man and orange, cinnamon and mint swirled in my nose, as I inhaled deeply.

TJ finished opening my shirt and slipped it down my back. He guided me to his desk and maneuvered my ass to the center.

I sat down on the mahogany as TJ slipped my shoes off me.

He grabbed my cuffs and pulled my suit pants off with one quick movement. He then slipped between my legs and caressed my leg as he drew near. His fingers ran through the hair on my legs, static electricity snapped along my calf. He circled my knee and ran his thumbs along my inseam. His fingertips tickled my balls as he played along the leg holes of my underwear.

My tan flesh contrasted against the white Egyptian cotton. The golden brown hair that covered my body deepened my tan. I looked up at TJ's body; his black hair traced along his sculpted muscles and gave texture to the marble perfection.

TJ pushed me down onto his desk. He raised my legs and stood between them. He bent forward and stuck his tongue in my belly button. He swirled it around and followed my treasure trail south. Next he worked his tongue under the elastic waistband of my underwear.

I could feel his warm wet tongue plow through the coarse pubic hair. He worked lower, deeper and my swollen flesh rose like a compass seeking north. My mushroom tip touched his tongue as my hips humped his face.

His hands pulled the cotton down, over my back end.

I rose up and allowed the last line of defense to slip away.

He worked my briefs down my legs and as he worked them over my feet he pulled my socks off at the same time.

Lying bare on his desk, I felt his warm mouth kiss my knee. He licked up my leg and worked his way to my testicle.

His nose nuzzled my balls. His tongue traced down a furry sac to the rounded end. He circled the dangling orb, kissed it once, sucked it into his mouth, and swallowed.

My head fell back as I savored his pleasure.

He worked over one ball and then started on the other. His mouth worked down to my taint and started to explore the crease.

I raised my legs and spread them as wide as I could.

His tongue found easy access and circled my tight opening. He drooled, adding lube to my sphincter. His tongue probed and coaxed me to relax. He licked and drilled into me.

My hands fisted and relaxed as my whole body spasmed.

TJ rose and spat into his hand. He grabbed my cock with one hand and slipped his index finger between my cheeks. He wiggled in the gluts and slowly, gently entered me. He worked my body.

I held onto the edge of the desk and tensed my body. The tingle started at the base of my spine and flowed through my limbs. His slow gentle strokes quickened as his finger dipped in deeper and deeper.

TJ fingered my prostate gland.

My toes curled as I humped his fist. My ass rode his hand and demanded more.

TJ followed my body's request and stroked faster, he drove into me deeper.

I could feel my balls pull up tight along the side of my shaft. It wouldn't be long before an explosive release would occur. But before that could happen I hooked my leg on the edge of the desk and pulled myself up.

TJ pulled out of me and released his hold on me. He kissed me as my arms wrapped around him.

I worked my hands down his body and undid his belt. His zipper opened and the hook opened as well, sending his pants to the floor in a ring around his ankles.

A surprised look came over his face.

Before he could move I grabbed the waistband of his briefs and slid them down.

My foot reached up and pushed them down to his slacks. I glided him around and gently pressed him against the desk. I then willed him down as I had been just a few seconds ago. My wet cock pressed against his firm ass as I stepped between his legs. My hands played along his muscular legs. My hand caressed his balls, lifting them up as my cock explored underneath.

My hand grasped his hard erection and I milked him.

TJ reached over the side of his desk and pulled a drawer open. He pulled out a square packet and a small bottle.

"You will need this," he said, bringing the packet to his mouth.

He tore it open and offered the condom to me.

I took it and slipped it onto my cock. I flipped the top open on the bottle and poured out a palm filled with lube. I smeared it down my length and worked the rest over my fingers. I reached between TJ's cheeks and sought out his hole. My finger found the tender spot and greased it.

TJ moaned, low and deep.

I slipped in two fingers and stretched his tight opening.

"Stick it in," he said almost breathlessly.

I moved between his legs and glided my cock to his ass.

"So you think that I can fill your opening?" I asked him and ran the tip of my cock along his crease, up and down, exploring.

TJ rocked his hips, pressing his butt down on me.

"Please," he begged.

My eight inches found the spot and stayed there. I circled my hips, pressing forward as I rotated. My lube covered hand grasped his cock and slowly slid up the length. My other hand combed through his pubic bush and up his belly. I sunk in deeper, filling him up.

He raised his hips and spread his legs apart. His muscles relaxed as my mushroom-head entered and the rest of the shaft glided in.

My shaved balls pressed against his furry butt, tickling me. I pushed forward as TJ's ass slipped on his desk. My knees banged the side and bounced back. TJ moaned as I withdrew. My balls tingled. I drove inside again and moved him closer to the center of his desk. I climbed on his desk with one leg, resting my knee on the top as I drilled him.

His butt sucked me in to the hilt as his muscled milked me.

The earlier stimulation forced my body to seek release. I jacked his cock hard.

His testicles rose up as I pulled on him, my cock slipped along the underside of them.

Our pace and speed doubled, tripled, quadrupled, as my other leg rose onto his desk.

The desk creaked with my added weight, but we continued. I looked out the open window, wondering who was watching my interview.

TJ's head rose and noticed my gaze.

"Being on display makes it even more exciting," he muttered.

I plunged in hard and his head fell back. A huge pearl of pre-cum oozed out of his slit and joined the lube. I could take it no longer. I rode his ass hard, knocking the breath out of him with each thrust. The pressure built in my balls.

"I…I…I'm…" was all that escaped out of TJ, when I felt a hot wave of cum shoot out of his cock and streak across his hairy belly and chest. Rope after rope of cum lassoed his torso. The smell assaulted my nostrils and I felt my balls release. I pounded into him over and over, with each spasm of pleasure. My legs and arms went rigid and sweat slipped down my back and funneled into my crack. The orgasm wracked my body and my body teetered for a few seconds. Then, my limbs went limp and I collapsed on TJ's cum covered body. My mouth found his and the taste of semen passed from him to me and back again.

My pelvis continued to thrust into him, filling the condom to capacity.

I lay on top of him as my heart and breathing retuned to normal. I pushed up over him and asked, "Was that part of the interview?"

TJ laughed and replied, "The job was yours before that."

I didn't say anything.

"I'm serious," TJ went on. "I think you would fit in well here. What would it take to get you to say yes?"

TJ waited.

I slowly withdrew from him, shuddering as I did.

"I would love to work for you and your company," I said as I rolled off him and lay next to him on the desk.

"I hear a "but" coming," TJ said.

"No buts, except maybe yours," I joked, caressing it. "Seriously, the salary and benefits sounds perfect. The job seems to fit my skills and I would enjoy coming in to work everyday. Everyone I've met seems to love what they do, and working for you is going to be great."

"So, what do you still need?" TJ finally asked.

"A corner office," I replied with a grin.

TJ rolled onto his side and kissed me. He then shook my hand, and said, "Welcome aboard."

THE BASIC LESSON

Written by Nicholas Bowman

Forget romantic notions about playing music on street corners for the sheer joy of it. The typical passer-by sees a busker as little more than just another annoying obstruction on the sidewalk, another panhandler to ignore.

To be fair, there are people who show their appreciation by tossing some money into the hat. Perhaps for the performance, perhaps for that romantic notion. They tip the usual dollar or two. Sometimes even a fiver.

Others just see buskers as beggars, but will give because we're at least doing something to earn the donation – unlike, say, the homeless person begging on the same block for whom it might make the difference between getting a meal and going hungry yet another day. They're good for a couple of quarters at best.

Then there are those who will tip if you're cute or look good with your shirt off or both. They tip well, very well. Needless to say, I hit the gym for a couple of hours six days a week to play shirtless whenever I can.

The catch is I'm a CP bottom. The gym isn't exactly a place where you want to be seen with odd-looking marks on your bottom. I get enough attention what with the ink, the brand, the stripes, and the hardware.

But if I want to keep my muscles defined and the tips coming in, I can't skip too many workouts. And even though I go to the gym during off hours, there are still guys wandering in and out of the locker room while I'm changing or in the shower.

Obviously I check for marks and then whether it's worth a calculated risk or making it the off day for the week. By the second day, all but the most serious bruising is gone or gone enough to take a chance.

Not that there aren't ways to work around the more usual next-day red-marks. I can dress and undress facing out with my back and bottom to the lockers so that any marks will not be easily seen. Or I can opt for the Catholic school boy squiggle: wrap a towel around my waist before I drop my trousers or gym shorts.

Stan, one of the personal trainers at the gym, does that. He does his own workout and hits the shower afterwards often about the same time as I do. With pale blond hair, pallid skin, and light blue eyes, he looks great with or without a towel around his waist.

While Stan and I match for three percent body fat, thirty inch waists, and hours put into working out each week, he is more than three inches taller, twenty-five pounds heavier, and five inches thicker around the chest.

But then again I'm turned on by well-built, good-looking guys wearing towels around their waists. As long as the waist measures less than the chest, a terry-cloth towel will hug the curves of the bottom, highlight the hollows of the hips, and nicely tent over even the softest of cocks.

I never really understood why Stan and the others of the squiggle school bothered. The showers are prison style – just a large tiled room with a row of shower heads along two facing walls. Modesty around the lockers and the way to the showers seems odd when you're going to wind up showing what you've got once you're in the shower room. Stan's by the way is long, thick, and uncut.

Though in Stan's case the modesty towel might be something he thinks is more professional since he is one of the personal trainers there. When he finally asked me about my hardware he backed into the question by saying he hoped I wouldn't misinterpret his interest. He then surprised me by not asking whether piercing my cock hurt, but why did I choose an ampallang over a P.A.

OK, it should have occurred to me at that point that his interest in me was less than professional. But it's a mainstream gym and I assumed most of the guys who work or workout there are straight.

I found out how less than professional Stan's interest was one day when we were the only guys in the shower room. It was a couple of days after a session with a reform school strap that was so intense that I found it more comfortable to stand all the way on the subway trip from Washington Heights to the Lower East Side.

I skipped my workout the next day, but since I didn't see any welts the day after that, I hit the gym for my usual routine. Stan and I wound up working out at the same time, but not together, and hit the shower at the same time, which was fine until I stepped under the cascading water. What I forgot was that hot water sometimes causes welts to resurface.

A knowing sidelong grin slipped over his face. "You are so busted, man."

"Yeah, man, what can I say?"

But the embarrassment turned me on and Stan too. We both laughed uneasily and ignored each others hard-ons.

I was a little apprehensive when I ran into Stan a couple of days later, but he didn't refer to the shower incident nor did he seem to treat me any differently than he had before. I shrugged it off. It probably wasn't the most embarrassing thing he'd seen in the shower room.

A week after that, Stan and I wound up as the last two guys in the gym as it was closing for the night. After we were both dressed, he pulled me aside.

"There are ways of taking care of boys like you," he said.

He pushed me into a storage room before I could think of what to say and locked the door.

I panicked, pounded on the door, and yelled to be let out.

Then I remembered I had my cell phone. Not that I used it. Now I wanted to know what ways of taking care of boys like me he had in mind.

The storage room wasn't the most interesting of places – just a jumble of unmatched dumbbells, broken exercise machines, and a massage table with torn vinyl. I sat on the table and waited. And waited. And waited. Anticipation grew almost as fast as apprehension. What was he going to do to me? Or was he just going to leave me there overnight?

Two hours later, Stan finally unlocked the door.

"Oh, man, I thought they'd never leave."

He pulled me back into the locker room.

"Time to strip for action."

I looked at him while he opened a locker door.

"All the way, man. Let's see those marks."

The marks were long gone, but I got the idea, even though at this point I'd usually be called "boy". I put my shoulder bag into the locker, and peeled off all my clothes, piling them on top of the bag.

My cock was full, but not stiff, from my being naked in front of Stan who remained dressed in layers long and short sleeved tee shirts, jeans with a heavy leather belt, and sneakers. He was turned on too to judge from the sidelong grin on his face and the expanding bulge in his jeans.

But other than openly enjoying the view, he wasn't sending off any of the usual dom signals.

"Sir?" I said.

"Cut the sir shit," he said as he shut the locker door. "Just Stan will do." He snapped on a combination lock and spun the dial.

Well, now I was fucked. My clothes and cell phone were inside a locked locker. Unless I wanted to run around New York naked there was no way I was leaving the gym until Stan decided I was leaving the gym. As a dom signal it was clear enough.

"Now let's see if your workout is as good as you think it is."

He headed to the door of the locker room, but I hesitated.

"Well?" he said.

I followed. This was going to be a bit weird.

We walked out onto the gym floor, which was cold to my bare feet. Most of the overhead lights were off, but a few were still on and provided a dim glow, just enough to see the equipment before you bumped into it.

I was turned on and scared – what if someone saw us?

Stan lead the way over to a pair of multi station machines linked by a pair of overhead crossbeams with wide and close grip chin-up handles.

"OK, Miller. We're gonna alternate burpees and chin-ups. Twenty-five of each with a full range of motion. No cheating. Let's bang them out."

"What's a burpee?"

On the other hand, who said not getting into a typical dom/sub role-play didn't have its good points.

"Squat thrust with a push up in the middle."

Stan demonstrated a quick one. He wasn't a personal trainer for nothing.

"Right," I said and took a deep breath.

I thought that exercise was called a squat-thrust pull-up, but whatever it's called, I'd seen him do a handful of them at the beginning and end of each of his workouts. Though I don't think I ever saw him do twenty-five of them in a row.

"Come on." He unbuckled his belt. "What are you waiting for?" He slipped the belt out of the loops, doubled it, and snapped it against my bottom. It hit hard and it hurt. He was either very mean or completely new to it.

Nevertheless, it was dom enough for me. I started the first burpee, squatted down and thrust my legs back, when the belt landed hard on my bottom.

"Move your ass, man. Bang them out."

I pushed up quick, but got another stinging whack.

"*Full* range of motion."

I did a deeper push up, my chin grazing the floor, snapped my legs back before he could belt me again and stood, pausing just long enough to be whacked again.

He was definitely new to it. Not a clue that both you and your sub will last longer if you start soft and work up in intensity.

I jumped and grabbed the grip bars and chinned. And got another snap of Stan's belt.

"Full range of motion, man. No cheating."

I pulled up again, getting my chin as much above the cross beam as I could.

I dropped to the ground. "That's one, Sir."

He snapped the belt against my bottom again. "I said cut the sir shit."

"Yes, Sir."

OK, I deserved that whack by anyone's standards.

I squatted and quickly thrust back, but I was already going down into the push up before the belt landed, all but pushing my chin into the floor.

Up again, tucked my knees between my legs fast enough that the next swipe missed me altogether. But he caught me in the split second between getting up from the burpee and the jump to grab the chin up bars.

"That's two, you fucker," I said as my feet hit the ground from the chin up.

"That's more like it." I got another whack, but it was light and playful and didn't land anywhere that had been hit before.

I dropped into the squat thrust, responded to being whacked on the push up of the push up with a "fuck off", and didn't get another belt until I pulled myself up on the chin up.

I dropped to the ground. "That's three, motherfucker."

He laughed and hit me again. The stroke wasn't that hard, but he hit an already sore spot.

He kept my pace up over the next ten or fifteen burpee/chin up combos, though my cock went limp by the fifth combo. But by twenty, my body began to slow down in spite of our best efforts.

I felt the push-ups burn my triceps and shoulders; my quads ached from the squats; and neither my biceps nor my traps were able to get my chin to the bar. My glutes hurt from the belt and not a good hurt either. I was beginning to say "motherfucker" like I meant it.

Finally, I reached the end of the twenty-fifth chin-up, barely managing to say, "Twenty-five, motherfucker", because the polymeric component was catching up with me.

He belted me again. "Take a rest."

I was short of breath. My bottom hurt. My cock was soft and small. His looked like it might burst out of his jeans.

He ignored all that. Instead he set the lat pull down for the highest weight possible.

"OK. Grab hold of the bar."

I just looked at him. "You really want me to sit down, let alone pull that weight?"

"No. You're gonna stand. Like for a stiff-arm pull down."

I got the image. And of the next item on the agenda as well.

I thought a moment. "You're a sick prick, Stanitsky. Assuming you've been doing the usual one quarter strength you're going to hit my limit in about sixtry seconds."

"Get over here or I really will hit you full strength," he said. "You're just as much a wimp as the rest of guys who think they're really training when they're just goofing around."

I straddled the seat and grabbed the bar, bracing myself for the worst.

To my surprise, he more than took the hint. The blows from the belt were feather-light, barely a tickle, and aimed at the least bruised parts of my bottom. Nevertheless, twenty-five of them was pushing it.

"OK, take a rest."

The rest was one minute on the clock.

"OK. Twenty burpees and chin-ups." He snapped the belt in the air.

Right.

"And this time, we'll add to the stripes on your back."

The scars on my back were a gift from a real motherfucker. And I did break. Not that that stopped him either.

I dropped for the burpee, but not fast enough to please Stan, who did land the belt on my back – just heavy enough to feel. I received a lighter blow on my bottom as I came up from the push up. And another on the back before I jumped to grab the chin up bar.

On the other hand, the blow when I said, "One, motherfucker", was at full strength, but at least it was on my back.

After about five combos, I figured out his pattern: heavier on the back, lighter on the buttocks, but two blows to my bottom for every one on my back. He did try to aim for the less sore spots, but he wasn't too good about that. On the other hand, he adjusted the pace to just to the edge of what I could handle as the stress and fatigue built. I was feeling it in my back, chest, and legs.

But it was good enough for both my hormones and my endorphins to kick into action. My cock swelled, all but grazing the floor at the bottom of the push up.

I just made the twenty reps – definitely because of the belt – but my cock didn't go soft with that set.

"OK, take a rest."

The rest was sixty seconds on the clock.

"Grab hold." He snapped the belt in the direction of the lat pull down machine.

I got into position.

"Let's add to your stripes there."

He laid on twenty, evenly split between forehand and backhand. They hurt, but not much, and wouldn't scar.

"You like that, don't you, you sick fuck." Stan sniggered.

As if he didn't like this.

A minute later, he had me do a set of fifteen burpee/chin up reps. He had to lay the belt on stronger this time, and kept about two strikes to my bottom to every one on my back. My form was getting less and less perfect as hand-eye coordination deteriorated with each repetition.

The fifteen strikes to my bottom at the lat pull down machine were also divided two to one, and also stronger than the last round. I was getting more turned on. When, I wondered, would foreplay be over? Assuming this was foreplay. And assuming I had any energy left. I was riding on endorphins and pure stubbornness.

Somehow I staggered through a fourth set of ten reps. I was exhausted and my cock went soft again, barely coming to life for the ten swats, all on my bottom.

The final set wound up being five forced reps: Stan had to help me through the chin and more than just spot the thrust and the push up. He made the final five swats to my bottom count: hard, but controlled.

I held onto the bar, trying to catch my breath and store up enough energy for whatever was next. Which I hoped would be a nice nap.

"Let's see that ass," he said.

He put an arm around my shoulders and guided me over to one of the stretching tables. I braced myself against the top.

"Oh, yeah. That's nice and red."

Stan admired his handiwork, lightly running a finger around the marks. His finger circled around my bottom, slipping along a thigh and prodding the back of my balls. His other hand roamed around my hip and circled my cock. He held it for a moment while it swelled in his hand. He let go and gave my balls a quick light squeeze. I didn't believe my body could still respond after sixty-five burpee/chin up combos.

"You like it red, too, don't you?" he asked me, sounding really intense.

"You know it, man." I responded.

He ran his hands over the red marks, which burned, but it was a good burn. One finger found my hole, circled the rim slowly a couple of times, relaxing the muscle, before sliding in. He prodded. He stroked. He had me moaning and gasping. He pulled his finger out and checked my cock.

"Shit. You're that hard without touching it?"

A few moments later, I felt how hard he was as his cock rubbed my bottom. He gently moved the cheeks to get it aimed into the hole. I relaxed and let him glide in.

He kept one hand on the table beside me and the other on the small of my back. I gripped the table with both hands as he moved inside me, fast and slow, hard and gentle, circling and back and forth. I leaned forward, chest to the table, to let him get deeper inside me. He grabbed my waist and picked up the pace.

"I think I'm going to cum," I gasped.

"Not before I do, man," he responded warningly.

He grabbed my shoulders and rammed his cock as deep as he could again and again.

I shot my load with a groan. My spasms must have brought him off to judge from his grunt.

He relaxed on top of me, his weight pinning me down, trapping me on the table, my cum sticky against my body.

He got up off me and I rolled off the table. I watched his cock small inside the condom before he pulled it off.

He looked at the table. "Oh, shit. I should make you lick that off."

"Or just spank me for making a mess."

He laughed as he pulled his tee shirt off and used it to clean the table top.

I ran into Stan a couple of days later in the shower room. The marks were gone. Mostly. Not that I saw him look.

Instead he said: "Noticed you get a lot out of working out with a partner. I have room the same time next week."

THE COP AND THE JOGGER OR THE JOGGER AND THE COP

Written by Anonymous Cop and Christopher Trevor

PROLOGUE

"MMMMFFFFFF!!!!! GRRRRRFFFFF..." the jogging attired man grunted and sputtered behind the tight fitting and mouth filling gag as he struggled to no avail against the intricately tied bonds that held him to the chair he was seated on. "RRRRFFFF..."

He groaned miserably and strained his well-muscled chest against the wire-like ropes wondering how something like this, *something so awful, so dreadful* could have befallen him. The way he was tied was like no other bondage setting for a seated guy he had ever seen before, not even in some hard-core porn magazines and videos. Even in mainstream movies where a secret agent is captured or on super-hero TV shows where the hero wound up bound did he ever see a guy tied in the way he was at this moment. The guy who had so expertly captured him had done a very good job in securing him that was for sure. As much as he struggled, strained and twisted in the chair there was just no getting loose. In fact, if he didn't know better he would swear that the ropes seemed to get tighter as he struggled. Was that possible???

He heaved himself upward as much as he could and bounced the chair a bit, moving it a tad around the dank and musty scented room he was in. And where was this place? That was the million dollar question. *Where had he been taken???* During the few moments that his eyes had not been covered he knew, from what he had been able to see that he was nowhere near where he had been so easily captured. JEEZ! The wire-like ropes were tied over and over and around and around his folded arms, his upper chest and just under his broad shoulders, pinning him to the chair, the way the man who had captured him had ordered him to position as he had sat down. Another length of the wiry feeling twine was wound frighteningly around his neck and the slack of it tied off to the bonds around his chest. Every time he moved his head he would pull on the rope around his neck which would of course choke him. Best to keep his head still he figured, until he could find some way out of this infernal mess he had been thrust so unwittingly into. A few lengths of the wire-like bonds were looped intricately and in a complex fashion around his thighs, just under the jogging shorts he wore and the slack of that wire was fashioned expertly and tied just under his knees, keeping him pinned down to the chair, no way of raising himself up off the damned butt-plug that was wedged in his shit chute. How the fucker had laughed when he had plugged his goddamned hole, shitty thing to do to a guy he thought at the time, no pun intended. Every time he heaved himself up a bit to move the chair around in the hopes of loosening the bonds he treated himself to a feeling of pressure and being fuck-raped in his ass. And each time that butt-plug tormented his hole he grunted like a madman in pain and his semi-erect cock in his shorts dribbled pre-seed born of fear. Fear- that was putting it mildly- the bound man was feeling totally and entirely terror-stricken. Things like this were only supposed to happen in the movies or in erotic fantasies, *not in real life*. The ropes tied around his sneaker and sweat socked feet were tied off to the lower rungs of the straight-backed chair, a finishing touch in keeping him snug and secure, as his captor wanted him.

Even worse, he thought was the leathery taste of the gag filling his mouth. It was that contraption, a combination gag and blindfold which confounded him the most. Not being able to speak was bad enough, seeing as the gag part of the contraption had a dildo shaped plug attached to it, which filled his craw miserably. He involuntarily chewed on the leather device that filled his mouth and every time he swallowed he tasted it. The strip of leather over his mouth kept the dildo gag hidden but firmly entrenched. Not being able to see made this situation all the worse, all the more frightening. Being plunged into darkness was awful. And to add insult to this misery the dildo gag and blindfold were all one piece. When the man who had captured him showed him the device he said that it was his own creation. The poor captured guy could not have cared less if his captor had created the damned thing, he just didn't want to be the one gagged and blindfolded with it. But seeing (again, no pun intended) as he was in no position to argue he really had no choice in the matter.

The bound man stopped struggling for a moment to catch his breath. He had been at it now for a good half hour or so, by his best estimates that is. Given his position it was not all that easy to concentrate on the passage of time. With his head facing forward so as not to choke himself with the rope twined around his neck he listened intently. He did not hear his captor's van pulling up outside. For the moment that was a good thing. It was only at the times when the man who had captured him left him alone that he was able to struggle and try to escape. Now granted, since his capture he had only been left alone twice, once when the man had gone to get food and now when the man had gone to relieve himself, or so he said. The bound man wondered what he would do when the time came that *he* would have to relieve himself. Since his capture he only had to piss and the man who had captured him had allowed him that luxury, while being supervised, HUMILIATING! The need to go was just about at the overwhelming and boiling point now. He realized that he had not been permitted the luxury of a bathroom since his capture. The butt-plug in his hole kept him good and stopped up…for the moment.

He breathed evenly behind his gag and smelled his own sweat. Being blindfolded seemed to heighten his sense of hearing and he thanked God for that as he listened for the man's van. And when the man returned God knew what he would put him through next. The thing he had done with binding him to the back of the motorcycle had been just about as shitty a thing that anyone could do to someone. But done to him it had been; there was no getting around it. What a thing to do to a poor guy he thought. It was part of the reason he was feeling so damned exhausted at the moment. He shook his head a bit from side to side, trying in vain to maybe get the damned blindfold off. That way he could at least see what the fuck he was doing as he tried to get loose. He splayed his fingers out and wiggled them, reaching for the knots in the wiry ropes that were just out of his reach, so close and yet so far he thought miserably. He knew that the man tied him that way, with his fingers loose to tease him, sadistic fucker that he was.

"MMMMMM…" he moaned miserably when he was about to get started again trying to get loose and realized he was more than winded. The jog he had been taken on earlier would attest to that being winded feeling. He would have to wait a bit more to get his second or third wind this time…but those thoughts were cut short when he heard,

"Well come on you were doing so well there, I really thought you were going to get loose that time," the man's voice said, chilling the bound man to his core.

Behind his gag the bound man said, "MMMMFFFFFFF!!!" and his blindfolded eyes were suddenly filled with terror. SHIT!!! He had been there the whole time. He had tricked him. He had made sure to keep totally silent as his captive struggled. And being that all the bound man could smell was his own sweaty scent and the musty odor of the room he could not have deciphered the scent of the man's cologne. Or perhaps he didn't have cologne on this day. He had obviously driven away and then made his way back on foot and silently sat enjoying as he watched the spectacle of the bound man's futile struggles.

"Now you know the rules my pet, you know what I told you would happen if you *even* attempted to get yourself untied," his captor said, sounding as sane as any normal person.

That was what made him all the more sinister, disturbing and terrifying, the fact that he could appear to sound so reasonable in what he was putting his captive through.

"RRRMMMMFFFFFF, rhooooooooooo…" the bound up man pleaded, trying to say "No."

"Oh yes you do, when I first captured you I told you that any sort of uncooperativeness would be dealt with in a most harsh manner, translation, *with punishment*," the ominous sounding man said.

The blindfold section of the device was removed followed by the mouth filling dildo gag. Well, at least one of the dildos wedged in him was out now he thought as the one in his shit chute continued to torment him. The gag came out all moist and soupy looking, drenched with the bound man's saliva and chewed up in sections. As his eyes adjusted back to the light of the dank room he looked up at the man who had so easily captured him. With pleading in his eyes he watched as the man sucked the dildo shaped gag, eating the man's saliva and mouth taste off the device. His captor seemed to be in a state of ecstasy as he swallowed and literally gulped down what was on the dildo. Watching him the bound man squeaked out the words, *"Please, please, no, no…I-I didn't do anything…I didn't get loose man…"*

Putting the blindfold/gag contraption down on a nearby table the sadistic looking man said, "I know you didn't get loose and as a reward I'll tie you tighter next time, after I'm done punishing you…"

"OH GOD NO…NO…PLEASE MAN!!!" the jogging clothed bound man begged as he watched the man dressed as a cop take a round black leather paddle from a hook on a wall.

"I think, Officer Baker, that you still have not learned your lessons," the man dressed in a cop's full uniform and regalia said as he stepped to his captive. "But I'm here to continue doing my very best to teach you…"

With that the bound man, fear filled as he was clenched his teeth and ranted angrily, "FUCKER, what you've done is against the law an…" But then, his words were cut short as the police uniform clad man clocked him hard and harshly across the jaw.

"OOOOFFFFFFF…" the bound man gasped in shock and his head spun.

The punch had seemed to come out of nowhere, he hadn't even seen it coming. In a stupor he felt himself being untied but there was nothing he could do to defend himself as the man quickly bound his hands behind him. Seeing as the guy had picked a leather paddle the trapped man knew he was in for more spanking. His poor ass cheeks were burned and scorched already, another hundred swats just might get them bleeding he thought with terror…

When he climbed out of his stupor he found himself mortifyingly splayed over his captor's knees, his hands bound tightly behind him, looking down at the floor and the man's booted feet.

"B-boots, th-those goddamned boots, they aren't yours..." the tied man moaned, his jaw aching where he had just been clocked, clenched his teeth and held back his tears of misery.

"They're mine for the duration you fucking bastard," his captor chuckled and pulled the bound man's jogging shorts down in back, tucking them under the man's delectable and melon-shaped ass globes.

"OH GAWD, my poor ass," the bound man grumbled.

His ass cheeks were the color of a fire engine, a testament to all the spankings he had already endured in such a short period of time. Was it just yesterday evening he had been captured? Or was it two evenings ago? Perhaps three??? My God he thought! He could not remember at this point. The base of the butt-plug stuck embarrassingly and mortifyingly from his shit chute. The man laughed and grabbed the base of the device, giving it a few twists and turns, tormenting and teasing the bound man's ass walls and his pucker.

"OHHHHHHHH..." the captured man moaned at his captor's booted feet.

"Yeah, you like that you pig, you fucking pig, you like it, *you fucking love it,*" the man's captor said gleefully as he let go of the base of the butt-plug and raised his leather paddle high. "Just from the steely feel of your damned erection in your shorts against my legs tells me how much you love that thing in your hole."

"FUCK YOU Mister, do your worst to me, but FUCK YOU all the same," the bound man seethed and then screamed in pain as the leather paddle came crashing down on his upturned already reddened and seared ass cheeks.

"This is for your own good Officer Baker," the uniformed man said and again brought his leather paddle swinging down and connecting hard with the man's ass cheeks, and again, and again... and again,

"AAAAAAYYYYYYRRRRRRRR!!!!" the captive man screamed and started counting the swats being administered to him.

He knew that not to count could double the hundred swats he was to receive. He also knew that not to count properly could result in the man starting back at number one again. He could not risk that...the cop who had been captured and had his uniform stolen by the man who had captured him and now wore it knew that... Motorcycle Patrol Officer Robert Baker knew that very well... In the short time that he had been this man's captive *that much* he had learned and committed to memory. As he was swatted and as he counted out numbers, to keep from going completely crazy and to perhaps get his mind off the pain he was feeling at the moment he allowed his mind to wander. But not to wander too far as to lose count that is... The cop, minus his uniform, his gun and his boots thought back to how he had come to be in this mess that he now found himself in...and being constantly and methodically brutalized...both mentally and physically...

CHAPTER ONE: THE PARK

That damned jogger; he was up to something but what the fuck was it? Motorcycle Patrol Officer Robert Baker knew that something was wrong with the guy, his body language alone attested to that. The cop just couldn't figure out exactly what it was his instinct was trying to tell him. One of Baker's areas of patrol was the park around the reservoir, a five mile stretch which people used for jogging, rollerblading, bike riding, baby carriage pushing and just plain walking. And because of all this there were muggers, thieves, drug pushers, rapists and even pedophiles always on the prowl. So with those things in mind it was an area of concern for the local police. Officer Baker first spotted the jogger a couple of weeks ago; he wasn't one of the regulars, he was a new face and he just didn't look right somehow. The other joggers on the trail, both male and female seemed to avoid him. They would speed up to pass him or shoot off on a side trail to evade him. It was as if they sensed something uneasy in themselves when he was around. So the cop wasn't the only one who felt this about the jogger it would seem. He had stopped him once, but only to talk and since the jogger had done nothing wrong and the cop had nothing but his own personal suspicions there wasn't much he could do. The last thing Officer Baker needed was to have someone file a harassment complaint against him, especially now that he was trying so hard to make detective. As much as the officer enjoyed being on his motorcycle, the thought of not having to don the uniform everyday with its tight pants, high boots, heavy helmet and knee length dress socks and replacing it all with civvies, comfortable jeans, sweat shirts, sneakers and thick sweat socks was his heart's desire and hope.

When Officer Baker had stopped him the jogger could not have been friendlier or more cooperative. He was totally polite with his "Good afternoon Officer Baker", eyeing the cop's nameplate as he spoke with him, making small talk about things like the weather and the health benefits where jogging was concerned.

"Yes Sir Officer Baker, it is a good day weather-wise for jogging," the jogger said agreeably as he smiled amiably at the handsome cop. "Well, you have a good day now Officer."

And with that he jogged off, sweating and puffing as he went. He had said those things politely but the smirk on his face had left Baker with the feeling that the man was making fun of him somehow, sort of bringing him down. And needless to say it pissed the cop off and made him even more determined than ever to learn what the jogger was up to. Baker had wanted to ask the jogger if he was new in town, where he was originally from, perhaps that would have given him some sort of clue as to what the jogger was up to. He hadn't even been able to find out what the jogger did for a living. The guy had sprinted off too quickly; obviously he sensed the cop's suspicions. The cop also realized that during the very short discussion he'd had with the jogger he had not gotten the man's name. The jogger had gotten his however, thanks to his nameplate pinned to his uniform shirt.

"Probably pushing drugs," the cop said to himself. "Or worse…"

Catching the man in the act, whatever the illegal act was, would assure Baker of getting the detective assignment he so badly coveted. But his suspicions were just that, suspicions, hunches, but damn, he thought, hunches are what make good detectives.

Officer Baker felt that he somehow recognized the jogger when he had stopped him, but for whatever the reason he could not place him. The two men seemed to be of the same height and weight, with body builds almost exact. True, the jogger seemed slightly older than the cop and he also had less hair and different facial features, but otherwise they could have been brothers.

Then, night after night after that one time meeting, Officer Baker had taken to lying in wait for the jogger behind a grove of trees. The cop would park his motorcycle off on the side of the trees, the vehicle out of sight of any passerby, and then squat down beside some bushes watching the trail below. Tonight was the fourth time Baker had done this and this time he had decided to stay a bit longer. The cop was thinking that perhaps the jogger did whatever it was he did when it grew dark. He hoped that he hadn't dirtied the pants of his tan uniform squatting there in the bushes because he hadn't retrieved his other pair from the drycleaners. Not that it mattered since he had the weekend off and could get them the next day, but damn, he wanted to hold off sending this pair to the cleaners until he actually had to. Staking out the park at this time of night was overtime on his uniform and he realized it would get a tad funkier that was for sure. Thoughts of the promotion he would receive overplayed thoughts of his uniform becoming mussed however. As he squatted there in the bushes he was glad that he hadn't told any of his cop brothers about this, about the jogger, about his suspicions where the jogger was concerned. Baker figured that when he busted the guy he would be much decorated with awards, a promotion and honors.

"Damn," the cop said to himself as he moved about in the bushes, watching different deserted areas every few minutes. "This park is a little creepy at night...too damn many shadows and trees moving in the wind. I hope that fucker shows up tonight..."

He removed his helmet and placed it on a rock next to him and then squatted again to watch the trail. It was then that he saw the jogger...

"Holy shit..." Baker whispered when he saw his prey lying on his back on the ground.

The guy was lying under a tree about twenty feet from where Baker was squatting. From what the cop could see the jogger was unconscious. Baker got to his feet and walked quickly over to where the jogger was lying, taking his flashlight from his duty belt as he went. The cop flicked on his flashlight and scanned it over the grounds surrounding the jogger. No signs of blood anywhere the cop quickly saw, so perhaps this guy was a victim of an overdose rather than foul play. Standing over the prone form of the jogger Baker scanned his flashlight over the guy's face. He could tell that the jogger was breathing. His chest was moving up and down and he was taking small breaths through his slightly opened mouth. The cop then scanned his flashlight up and down the jogger's arms, looking for track marks, finding none. Just great, the cop thought, I wanted to bust him for an illegal act and I'm going to wind up taking him to a hospital.

"Hey buddy, can you hear me?" Baker said, pressing the toe section of one of his boots against the jogger's leg.

"Mmmmmm…" the jogger moaned softly.

"You okay there bud?" Baker asked squatting down on his haunches next to the jogger and slipping his flashlight back into his belt, ready to reach for his radio to summon an ambulance. "Hey, can you hear me?"

The jogger was clad in his usual attire of athletic clothing, a black tee shirt with white stripes on it, matching thigh length shorts and black and white sneakers with white sweat socks tucked down into them.

"I-I, wha-what happened?" the jogger grunted, opening his eyes and staring up at the cop. "H-hey there Officer Baker…what are you doing here?"

Baker smiled and said, "I just might ask you the same thing bud. You mind if I help you into a sitting position there?"

The cop slid a hand under the jogger's neck. He gently hoisted the guy into a seated position on the ground, one arm around him as the jogger lolled his head around and he never noticed the cloth in the jogger's hand, not until it was too late.

"You okay?" Baker asked and he could smell the scent of cologne wafting off the guy.

"G-guess I conked out or something," the jogger said and as Baker squatted there holding the guy up the jogger suddenly pounced.

Before Baker knew what was happening the jogger was up and on him, pressing a white cloth that smelled sickly and sweet against his nose and mouth.

"H-HEY, what the fruck…" Baker snarled as the cloth was pressed hard over his nose and filled his mouth. "GGRRRRFFFFFFF!!!!"

The cop struggled like a madman, reaching for his holstered gun as the jogger was suddenly straddling him, one hand behind his big neck, the other pressing the horribly scented cloth against his face. As he struggled crazily Baker found that it was now *he* himself who was lying on the ground, the jogger's knees pressed against his forearms, no chance of getting his gun or even his radio to summon backup. The cop realized that for some reason the jogger had planned this and he had been had.

"Take it cop, inhale, inhale, *fucking inhale,*" the jogger seethed.

Baker's booted feet kicked and lashed out against the concrete ground as he slowly lost consciousness. He knew what the scent was that he was being made to inhale, chloroform. Fuck, fuck, he had definitely been had the cop said to himself miserably. He struggled some more to no avail. The jogger took the cloth away from the cop's face, clocked him twice across the jaw, getting some "OOOOOFFF" sounding grunts out of the cop and then meanly chloroformed him again.

"MMMM…" Baker moaned behind the cloth against his face.

The jogger held the cloth tightly again against the cop's nose and mouth. Stunned as he was from having been clocked on the jaw Baker simply inhaled. A few moments later the jogger again took the cloth slowly from the cop's face. He looked down at him. In a stupor Officer Baker looked up into the eyes of the jogger, eyes that were filled with what appeared to be sadistic glee and vicious merriment.

"WH-what the fuck?" the cop whispered as his head spun and he saw the jogger helping himself to the handcuffs and gun on his duty belt.

"Still awake huh Officer Baker?" the jogger asked and held up the white cloth.

"No, no," the cop pleaded as he was dosed a third time. "RRRMMMMFFFF..."

Leaving the now unconscious cop laying there locked in his own handcuffs, his wrists behind him; the jogger sprinted to where Baker's motorcycle was. That was the first thing that he needed to make disappear, then of course Officer Baker himself. The jogger rolled the motorcycle quickly past the unconscious cop and up into the back of a van he had parked behind and down the trail.

A few short moments later the jogger was carrying the still unconscious cop over one shoulder, his arm looped around and just under the back of Baker's knees and just above his high boots, toward his van. The jogger was wearing the cop's helmet, not wanting anyone later to find any evidence of the cop's capture. The jogger deposited the cop in the back of the van along with the motorcycle, tied his booted feet tightly together and slammed the back doors of the vehicle shut.

"And we're off," the jogger laughed as he got behind the wheel of the van, Baker's gun and his switched off radio in his belt.

As the jogger drove of with his prize the park was again silent, no sign whatsoever that a cop had just been so brutally captured and sprinted off with.

CHAPTER TWO: THE EXCHANGE

A couple of hours later the van pulled onto a deserted country road and eventually into the yard of a medium sized house with a large barn-like structure adjacent to it. The jogger backed up to the door of this structure, opened it and then unlocked the rear of the van. He looked in at the still unconscious cop bound and foot. The jogger pulled the cop out, easily flipped him over his shoulder and brought him inside the building, dropping him on the floor. It was a large building with stone walls and looked deceptively dilapidated, however, it was anything but. The jogger had spent a lot of time fixing the structure to his liking and although it had the appearance of a large prison cell it was far more than that; it was a dungeon unlike no other. Next, the jogger retrieved the cop's motorcycle and parked it in another section of the building, out of sight. He returned to the still out-of-it cop, gazed down at him and laughed.

"Welcome to your new home Officer Baker," he said.

The jogger took the handcuffs off the cop's wrists and then cuffed just one of the officer's wrists to a metal ring embedded in the floor. He carefully removed the cop's duty belt and placed it along with the gun and radio he had already taken earlier on a table nearby. If the cop had been awake he would have been able to move but that was about all since one wrist was securely fastened to the floor. The jogger stood looking at the muscular shape of his prisoner, imagining all the fun times he was about to have. He knelt down beside the cop and slowly pulled off one and then the other of the tall, black leather boots, but even this action failed to rouse the cop from the chloroform induced stupor he was under. Still kneeling next to his captive the jogger gave in to a strong and suddenly unusual urge to massage the cop's feet. The cop was wearing long, black nylon dress socks and the jogger, for some reason, could not resist the temptation of massaging those strong masculine feet. At one point he even raised one of the cop's black socked feet to his mouth and sucked on the toes through the funky scented dress sock.

"Ah," he thought to himself. "Cop feet are so delicious.

Then, knowing that the cop would be out for at least another hour the jogger left him there and went into the house next to the building where he had himself a cold beer and some food.

Eventually Officer Baker began to come around; it was a slow process and it left him with a throbbing headache and a bitter taste in his mouth. He moaned softly and went to rub his head when he realized he couldn't lift his hand. He opened his eyes fully and found himself on a stone floor with one wrist chained to a steel ring.

"What the fuck!" the cop said.

The jogger, sitting nearby in a chair had watched the cop come to.

"Ah, my pet," he said. "Welcome back to the real world. Undoubtedly you're feeling kind of nauseous right now, but don't worry, that's just the chloroform I used on you; you'll be back to normal soon."

"What the fuck is going on? Uncuff me you shit-head!" the cop rasped, recognizing the jogger and remembering his suspicions of how the guy was up to something.

He had been up to something alright, he had been intending to capture a damned cop, and Officer Baker found to his woe, that he was the cop the jogger had captured.

"Damned asshole, you can't just kidnap a cop like this!" Baker went on, seething through clenched teeth. "Who the fuck are you and what the hell do you want?"

"Two questions Officer Baker and I didn't even give you permission to speak," the jogger said. "But I can understand your confusion, so this time I will forgive you. Who am I, you want to know? Obviously you don't recognize me. Ah well, maybe you'll remember eventually."

"Yeah, I did think you looked familiar when I spotted you jogging," the cop replied. "But damned if I know why. I do know that if you don't let me go right now you'll be known in prison by the number they'll assign you there."

"Well my pet, we'll see," the jogger went on. "But for now you can call me Sir. As for what I want, ah, that's a good question, a very good question, and you will find out all in good time. For now let's say that I just want to spend some quality time with you, as the shrinks say. Eventually all will come clear to you. But what I want right now is your uniform, so kindly take it off. Notice that I've helped you a little by removing your boots, and such good quality boots they are. The police department outfits its officers with the best, I must say."

"Are you out of your fucking mind?" the cop practically shouted now. "No way in hell am I taking off my uniform. You're fucking sick man."

"Well I suppose I could force you to do it," the jogger said, picking up the cop's weapon and pointing it at him. "But putting a bullet in you is the last thing I want to do- at least at this point in our relationship. Or, I could give you another dose or two or three of chloroform and then just strip you myself. Yes, that might be fun, handling/fondling your strong cop body while I remove your clothes. Or better yet I could just zap you with the taser gun I took from your motorcycle saddlebags. I understand that one blast from it really hurts like the devil. It's up to you my pet, which do you want?"

"Fuck you, I'm not your pet you asshole," the cop ranted but the thought of getting hit with the taser was enough to make him concede.

He had seen what happened to a guy who had been tased and it wasn't pretty.

"Okay, okay, but how the fuck can I strip out of my uniform when I'm cuffed like this?" the cop asked.

"Well Officer, you can do it in sections," the jogger instructed. "Start with the items below the belt, your socks, and your uniform breeches. You have one free hand which can effectively do the job. Start with your socks on those beautiful cop feet of yours."

The cop looked down at his socked feet and then up at the jogger.

"Fucking pervert," the cop muttered but he lifted one leg and pulled down the thin, black sock covering his foot; first one foot then the other.

He placed each item of clothing next to him in a pile. Then, with his hand and fingers trembling he unbuckled his belt, unzipped his fly and pulled down his uniform pants, which he worked off his legs and placed near his socks. He sat there on the floor wearing only a pair of white briefs and the top part of his uniform.

"Underwear too Officer," the jogger said commandingly.

"What are you some kind of crazy voyeur?" Baker asked miserably. "Looking at my cop-sized balls and dick gonna give you a cheap thrill you creep?"

"The briefs Officer and quit the backtalk or..." the jogger said and held up the taser gun.

"SHIT! Okay," the cop railed and stripped off his tight-whities, adding them to the pile.

He sat there with his crotch exposed and felt more embarrassed than he had ever felt before in his life. The jogger admired what he could see, a cock that was semi hard but already over six inches long and nicely thick. He tossed the key to the cuffs to the cop and ordered him to undo his wrist. The cop thought to himself that this was finally his chance; once he was free he would rush the bastard and overpower him. But after he had freed himself he looked up to find the jogger pointing the taser directly at him. Fuck, fuck, no way was he going to chance getting zapped by that. Another chance would come. So, he reluctantly removed the tan uniform shirt, tie and his tee and placed them in the pile as well. The cop was totally naked now.

"Very good Officer," the jogger laughed. "Now cuff your wrist back and toss me the key.

The cop, with no choice in the matter did as he was told.

"That's a good boy," the jogger said with a grin as he held the key in hand. "See, if you cooperate nothing bad can happen to you. Well, maybe that's not one hundred percent true, but trust me, it is far better that you cooperated because the punishments can be far, far worse if you don't."

The jogger picked up the cop's discarded uniform and took it to the table where his boots and duty belt already sat.

"I always wanted to be a cop and wear a sexy uniform," the jogger said. "Now is my chance. And especially since we seem to be the same size so everything should fit."

The cop stared at the jogger, said, "You're fucking weird, you sicko!"

The jogger removed the jogging gear he was wearing from his sneakers to the heavy sweat socks to the shorts, jersey and even his jockstrap. He picked up the cop's white briefs and pulled them on over his muscular legs and up to his crotch and ass.

"Mmmmm," he said. "Nice and they fit perfectly. Fuck, it feels awesome wearing your under shorts my pet."

He walked past the cuffed cop, parading his body like he was a model on a runway.

"Fucking unbelievable, truly sick," the trapped cop murmured.

Next the jogger pulled the cop's socks onto his own feet, long, thin black socks that climbed up almost to his knees. There was something really sexy about Officer Baker in that he opted for these thin black socks with his uniform, dress socks really, rather than thick sweat socks that so many of the officers chose to wear under their boots. Then came the flared, tan uniform breeches. The jogger then lovingly picked up one of the boots and to the surprise and disbelief of the cop he placed the opening of the boot against his face. He breathed in deeply the aroma left by the cop's foot after a long day of having worn it. The jogger did this with both boots before pulling them on his feet and then once again modeled for the bewildered cop.

"When I saw that we had the same size ten and a half sized feet I knew I had to wear these boots," the jogger chuckled. "They fit perfectly and feel so damned good."

Finally came the uniform shirt which the jogger buttoned up and then tucked into the breeches before zipping up and strapping on the duty belt with all the cop gear on it. Smiling, he put on Baker's tie.

"Perfect," he said. "Fucking perfect! Now I'm the cop in charge and you are the prisoner. Perfect. But wait, it isn't fair. I mean, here I'm in your clothes and you have nothing to wear. Hmm, I suppose it's only right that you wear my clothes now. I don't want you going around naked all the time. Since I've become the cop you have to become the jogger. Yes, that's it. Here, start with my jockstrap."

He tossed the jockstrap to the naked man but the cop batted it down.

"No fucking way am I wearing that damned thing," the cop reeled. "You pervert, sicko, asshole!! No way!"

But then suddenly a bolt of pain hit the cop and he screamed. Pain was tearing through him like he had never felt before in his life, electricity searing through his entire body, it was excruciating pain. He curled up in a ball on the floor, screaming for it to stop, begging for no more, and pleading for it to stop.

"Ah yes, it is good to see that this taser works as efficiently as I thought it would," the jogger commented. "Now listen to me, either you do what the fuck I say or you'll get more of this treatment."

As he spoke he continued firing the taser at the cop.

"Do you understand boy?" the jogger asked.

"Yes, yes…anything, just turn the damned thing off," the cop screamed. "PLEASE, OH GOD, I'll wear your clothes, anything you want, only stop it!!!"

And so the once in charge cop did as he was told and dressed in his captor's jogging outfit- first the jockstrap, then the socks, shorts, shirt, and sneakers. Their roles were now completely reversed; the jogger had become the cop and the cop had become the jogger.

CHAPTER THREE: THE LEATHER PADDLE

The cop stood there in the jogger's clothes, still tingling from the effects of the taser blast. He was trembling a little and almost didn't catch the handcuffs the jogger tossed at him.

"Okay my pet, cuff one wrist, then hands behind your back and cuff the other one," the jogger commanded. "I'll be watching closely so you better do it right."

The frustrated and terrified cop knew he had no choice so he cuffed his wrists as ordered. The jogger went to inspect and closed the cuffs one or two notches tighter on the cop's wrists.

"Now my pet, I think you need a little punishment for not doing what I ordered the moment I ordered it," the jogger said, holding the cop's upper arm in a firm grip. "From now on when I say for you to do something, no matter what, you will do it- IMMEDIATELY! Is that understood?"

The cop just stared blankly at his captor as the man let go of his arm...

The jogger sat down in the chair the cop had been tied to and ordered his captive over to him. Standing before the seated jogger the cop was unprepared when he was grabbed and flipped, landing on his stomach on the lap of the jogger.

"You've been a naughty boy Officer Baker, and now you have to be spanked," the jogger announced.

The cop could not believe this was happening. He could not believe any of it was happening. He had been kidnapped, brutalized, stripped, made to wear another man's clothing and now he was about to be spanked like a misbehaved child. The cop truly could not believe it when the jogger produced a thick leather paddle and gently rubbed it over his upturned ass.

"Now let's get down to business," the jogger said laughingly. "You will count the blows as you get them and if you miss a count then I will start all over again."

"OH GOOD GOD," the cop said from his position and lifted his head a bit.

"But first my little pet I want you to kiss this paddle to show just how much you love it," the jogger ordered.

The frazzled captured cop wanted to swear and tell his captor off but the leather paddle was thrust down and in his face. It was shoved right up against his quivering lips and without thinking he kissed it.

"Good boy," now remember to count out loud and to thank me for administering the punishment," the jogger said, raised his arm and brought the paddle down hard on the cop's bare ass.

"AAAHHHHHHHH!!!" the cop cried out. "Fuck man that shit stings!"

"Now, now Officer, that is not the correct response," the jogger said. "Of course it stings, it's supposed to. But I want you to count out and thank me for doing this. The sooner we begin and you do it correctly the sooner it will end. Now, we'll try again."

And with that the man leveled another hard blow against the poor cop's ass.

SMACKKKKKKKK

"AAARGGHHHHHH" the cop cried out. "ONE, thank you..."

"No, no Officer," the jogger admonished Officer Baker yet again. "How can you be so damned stupid? You must love the feel of this paddle. You know that you must address me correctly. I am in charge here; I am your superior so you must address me accordingly. Call me Sir when you thank me. Do you understand?"

"Yea, yeah, okay...okay...I'll do it..." the cop responded.

And then SMACCCCKKKKKKK another blow on the cop's poor ass.

"Address me correctly you stupid moron, or the punishment will be even worse," the jogger seethed and swatted the cop's ass again.

"Sir, yes SIR...I'll do what you say SIR," the cop bellowed.

And so it began, hard steady blows alternating on the cop's ass cheeks. And the captive cried out the number and his thank you after each blow. He accidentally skipped number twenty-one and after being once again berated for being stupid, the entire process began again.

"OOOOOOOOOWWWWWWWWWWWWWWW!!!!" Officer Baker snarled as his ass cheeks were swatted harder and harder it seemed with each blow from the leather paddle. "YOU FUCKER, my ass feels like its been turned to minced meat!"

"It's starting to look like that as well Baker," the jogger laughed and swung the paddle hard again, bringing it down three times in fast succession on the cop's upturned ass cheeks.

"OOOOHHHHHHHRRRRRRR, sixty, sixty-one, sixty two, and FUCK YOU!!!" Baker roared, tears of tortured pain spilling from his eyes.

"I'll allow the swearing for now Officer Baker, seeing as what I'm putting you through warrants it perhaps," the man who had captured the cop said sadistically. "But the next time I discipline you, you'll be thanking me instead. And don't think for a second that you won't. With all that I have planned for you, you will come to do whatever the fuck I say."

The cop prayed that he would not lose count again. To have to start again at number one and then endure yet another hundred swats was unthinkable. At the seventieth swat the jogger stopped paddling the cop.

"OHHHHHHHHHH, th-thank you, thank you…" Baker grumbled, sweating and trembling like a leaf over his captor's lap.

"Oh we're not done yet my pet," the jogger chuckled, calling the cop by a nickname, and a degrading nickname at that. "Your ass cheeks are welting up in spots and I don't want to have you bleeding. I'll take measures to make sure you don't bleed and then I'll administer the last thirty swats. A hundred is your magic number Officer Baker."

The man laughed again and that was when he inserted the butt-plug into the cop's anal canal. The cop screeched and bellowed as the thing entered him. He screamed bloody murder as the jogger then gave the butt-plug a few twists and turns. He put the paddle down on the floor, right under the cop's face as his head dangled at his captor's booted feet. The next thing Baker felt was aloe cream being smeared over and over his reddened and welted ass cheeks.

"Mister, what the fucking fuck are you doing?" the cop asked, sounding incredulous.

"This will insure that you don't bleed my pet," the jogger explained, his jiggling fingers filling sections of the cop's ass cheeks as he slathered and greased them. "I want to work you over as much as possible, but having to rush you to an emergency room does not figure in my plans."

"JEEZ, thanks for small favors," the captured cop replied sarcastically and breathlessly.

Then, the cop was screaming in pain yet again as the ass swatting began once more…

At the count of one hundred the jogger in the cop's uniform stopped and admired the swollen, red ass of his captive.

"Ah, that was most enjoyable," the jogger said. "I do hope you learned something from that my pet. You are to do exactly what I tell you to do, with no backtalk or hesitation. If not, then more and more severe punishment will be meted out on you. Now do you understand boy?"

"Sir, yes SIR," Officer Baker responded.

"Good boy," the man said and flipped the cop from his lap down to the stone floor. "Stay there for a minute boy, while I get some more salve for that ass of yours. You earned a little relief."

The cop was too exhausted to move so he just lay there. The jogger returned and began rubbing the soothing salve onto the cop's bruised and reddened ass.

"I must admit my little pet, that you do have a beautiful and muscular ass. Must be a result of riding on that motorcycle all day."

The jogger grabbed the cop by his feet and dragged him unceremoniously over to the metal ring on the floor. He attached a heavy ankle cuff to the cop and secured him to the ring.

"Okay boy, rest up," the jogger said. "I think we'll be going for a ride soon and I want you ready for it."

CHAPTER FOUR: MOTORCYCLE JOGGING

The poor, red assed cop just lay there, exhausted and weak. What the fuck is this all about he wondered. Why is this happening? Why has that jogger kidnapped me? WHY ME??? But it soon became too much for him to think about and against all logic he fell asleep. The jogger, now dressed as a cop, returned later and watched as his captive slept soundly on the cement floor. The cop's muscles expanded and deflated as he breathed in and out. It was a pleasant sight and part of the jogger wanted to reach down and caress this muscular man on the floor. But there was much still to be done and the jogger could see no reason why he should allow this police officer to relax at all. No, he had to break him down. He had started already in breaking the officer's resolve and now he would continue. He took a pitcher of ice cold water and poured it over the cop's head. Officer Baker awoke with a start, a scream and a bedazzled look on his face.

"What the fuck? Where am I? I…" the cop began but when he saw the jogger standing over him in his uniform he remembered what had happened and began to curse at the jogger like a marine.

"Ha, ha," the jogger laughed. "It's good to know that you still have some fight and spunk in you my pet. I like that in a slave, my slave."

"Your slave?" the cop ranted. "Fuck you man, I'm not your slave, you asshole! You're in such deep shit now that you'll never get out of prison. Now, uncuff me and let me the fuck out of here."

"Oh dear Officer, you do so scare the shit out of me…NOT!" the jogger responded mockingly. "I think it is you who is in deep shit my pet, not me. But as I said, it's good to know you still have some resistance in you. Now my pet I know it's hard for you to tell having been, shall we say, locked up in this building for so long, but believe me it is an absolutely fantastic day out there. Wonderful warm spring weather. Perfect for a ride through the country. What do you say; do you want to go for a ride with me?"

The cop, leery of what his captor might be planning nevertheless thought that if they left the building where he was being held then he might stand a better chance of escaping. And if nothing else at least he might get a bearing as to where they actually were. So he agreed, saying, "Yeah, I'd like that."

"Good boy," the jogger said. "Now I'm sure that you're probably thirsty from all your efforts so I've brought you some water. Don't want you all dehydrated my pet."

With that the jogger produced a bowl of water and placed it next to the cop's head. The cop stared at it and realized that yes indeed he was thirsty and he knew that the only way he could get the water was to lap it up like a dog…another humiliating act he would have to perform in front of this weirdo who momentarily controlled him. So he sighed miserably and lowered his head to the bowl. He began lapping up the cool refreshing liquid.

The jogger smiled with delight as he watched the cop and listened to the slurp, slurp of his tongue trying to get as much water into him as he could. Finally, the cop finished the bowl and looked up at his captor.

"Okay my pet, you've done very well," the jogger said. "What do you say we go for that ride now?"

With that he removed the ankle cuff from the cop's leg and helped him stand, the cop's wrists still cuffed behind him. Having been on the cold floor and in one position for so long the cop had a little trouble adjusting to standing and walking, so the jogger led him around the floor a few times, holding him tight by his upper arms as the cop walked until his balance returned. Next, the jogger unlocked one of the handcuffs from the cop's wrist, leaving the other cuff dangling on his other wrist, but before his captive could do much he pointed the taser gun at him. Shuddering, the cop simply stood there, a blank look on his face.

"I'm relying on you not to try anything funny my pet," the jogger said. "I'd hate to have to use this gun on you again. Now, hold out your hands in front."

The cop did as ordered and the jogger locked his hands in front of him this time. Next, the jogger tied a strong length of rope to the cuffs. The rope had a good ten foot lead to it and holding that the jogger led the cop out of the building.

The cop was dazzled by the bright sun when they stepped outside and it took him a few moments to adjust. He walked along behind the jogger as the man led him by the rope. Then, the cop realized that they had stopped in front of his own motorcycle, parked by the building.

As the jogger adjusted the helmet on his head he chatted with his captive.

"I've been practicing on this bike while you slept away my pet," the jogger said. "It's a great Harley. The city does indeed provide only the best for its officers. You are lucky. Now, I think we should go for that ride, but as you obviously know, this bike only seats one, so I guess there isn't room for both of us. And since I have the key I suppose I'll be the one to drive. You, my pet will have to jog along after me. But I'm sure you'll enjoy seeing the countryside."

With that the jogger tied the other end of the rope to a metal bar on the seat of the motorcycle. The cop realized then what was going to happen and with his eyes opened in total terror he tried to pull away, but between the cuffs and the rope there was not much he could do.

The jogger then mounted the motorcycle and started the engine.

"You ready my pet?" he asked loudly as the machine roared to a start.

"Shit, shit, *shit...*" the cop muttered, his voice not heard by the jogger due to the roar of the motorcycle's engine.

The jogger drove out of the yard slowly and the cop had no choice but to walk alongside. But once they reached the country lane the jogger picked up speed and soon the cop found himself jogging to keep up. They only went about five miles total, a distance the cop often covered when he went for his weekend runs, but this was different. On open stretches the jogger would rev the engine and increase the speed, causing the cop to run as fast as he could to keep from falling and being dragged, but then the bike would slow down and the cop would lapse into a jogging mode again, catching his breath, inhaling the bike's exhaust, making him cough at the same time. The cop had hoped to get a bearing on where they were but his total effort was in staying on his feet and keeping up so he saw little of the farm country where they were riding. In addition he could smell more and more of the exhaust fumes from the bike. Because he was now directly behind the exhaust pipe the scent tended not only to make him cough, but made him feel dizzy as well. The cop didn't know where they were or how far or how long they were gone as his entire mind and attention was on just surviving. The driver it seemed knew the area however and had simply made a circular run, returning to the building where they had started. The jogger thought to himself that this should wear that asshole cop out enough so he doesn't try anything funny. Ha, ha, what a wonderful punishment this was.

CHAPTER FIVE: COOLING DOWN

Baker couldn't believe that he was still on his feet when they finally pulled back into the yard of the house and the rope attaching him to the motorcycle was removed. He was exhausted, his feet hurt in his captor's old sneakers and his legs felt as if they were encased in cement. He stumbled into the room being pushed by the maniac who had captured him. Once inside Baker collapsed on the stone floor, panting for breath, gasping for air.

"Ah, my poor little cop boy, my pet is hot and tired," the jogger teased. "Well, I guess you've earned another drink of water for all that exercise you just completed. You did well boy, but I think you'll improve on future runs."

Baker groaned when he heard that. No way could he go through that again; he needed to get out of this mess. But now he was too beat to do anything but lay there. The real jogger went into the next room and came back with a bowl filled with water but before he let the cop lap it up he uncuffed his hands and then quickly re-cuffed them behind his back. The cop didn't even try to resist, he was that exhausted.

"Okay boy, enjoy your drink," the jogger said.

Baker crawled to the water and lowered his face into the bowl. Damn it felt great as he used his tongue to lap and sip the water and lessen his need for the liquid. He stayed at it for some time, pushing the bowl around with his mouth as he tried to get as much into him as he could. Finally he heard, "Enough boy, get over here. I have something for you to do." Baker knew better at this point to argue or even hesitate so he crawled to where his captor sat, his legs sprawled out in front of him.

"Ah boy, that ride was invigorating, I do enjoy my new motorcycle," the jogger said and the cop seethed.

His motorcycle? The jogger's motorcycle??? It was Baker's motorcycle, and somehow the cop would get it, and his uniform, and his boots back. He lustfully thought of his duty belt and his gun.

"But because of our ride just look how dirty and dusty my new boots got during that ride," the jogger scoffed. "I want you to lick them clean boy, don't let me see a speck of dust on them when you're finished."

Baker knew he had no choice but to obey, but the thought of having to clean his own boots with his tongue while this fucker wore them was humiliating and discouraging. He thought to himself that when this was over and he was free again he would throw those boots away; he could never put them on his feet again, not after this bastard, whoever the hell he was, had worn them. And what was even worse was that he had to lick them clean, tasting the dirt and dust of the road and swallowing it down. What could be more debasing than having to tongue clean the boots on another man, especially, when in reality the boots were actually your own?

Baker sighed and bent down to do the job. He worked on the boots for over an hour and when he finished they once again had that clean, shiny look to them. He fell back on his side and looked up at his tormentor.

"Not a bad job boy," the jogger said as he looked down at his boots and then at the cop on the floor. "Later when you have some spare time you can spit shine them for me. You'd like that wouldn't you boy?"

Baker said nothing.

"Boy, you still look all hot and sweaty," the jogger went on. "Not used to good old fashioned exercise I see. Well, I have another treat for you which should help cool you down a little. Stand up and follow me."

The man took the cuffed cop to a wooden horse like device and had the cop bend over it, his legs spread wide. With quickness and skill the jogger deftly and securely tied the cop's ankles to the legs of the horse and then used leather straps to lash the cop's upper body to the device. It was very effective and the cop was fastened securely. Then, the man produced a thick leather collar and locked it around the cop's neck and, using a heavy chain, pulled it down and locked it to a ring embedded in the floor. It seemed the jogger had those rings embedded in the floor in a lot of places where he was being held the cop thought. This secured the cop even more and all be could do was stare down at the floor below him. Next, a black rubber ball gag was inserted and strapped tightly in the cop's mouth.

Baker was sweating again. He could smell the rank odor coming from his own body and feel the sticky, sweat stained jogging outfit clinging to his muscular body. His feet, slightly swollen from the run, ached inside the thick sweat socks and sneakers. But worse was his captor's jockstrap which he had been forced to put on way back when he was first taken prisoner. It itched and his balls sweated inside and, worse, his cock seemed to be in a perpetual state of semi-hardness, which confused the poor officer of the law all the more. Baker swore to himself that he would reap revenge on this sadistic bastard if it was the last thing he ever did. He sensed his captor behind him but once again the man moved so silently that the cop was surprised at his return.

"Well my little pet," he said. "You really do look all worn out and I admit it is a little hot in here. So, I prepared something to help cool you down."

He then stood in front and lifted the cop's head up just enough so that the officer could see what he held in his hand.

"Oh my God, no, no…NO…" the cop screamed through his gag, but of course it came out only as a muffled roar.

"Let me explain," his captor said. "This is an extra strength condom; actually it is two of them, one inside the other. What I did was fill it with water and then tied it off at the top and froze it. Well, I'll level with you, its more than just plain water. It has a substance in it which will keep the ice hard for longer than it normally would last. Of course it will still melt, but just not as quickly as usual. It's only about ten inches long but I'm sure that's enough to cool you off inside. I only hope you'll enjoy the sensation my little pet."

His tormentor went to the rear, the cop's ass sticking up high in the air, and then pulled down the jogging shorts. The cop screamed through his gag and struggled to break free but of course to no avail. The jogger slid the butt-plug out of the cop's hole and then with one forceful thrust the iced dildo was shoved up the cop's already very sore asshole. The jogger used some duct tape to secure it so it would not pop out. The cop screamed louder and louder through the gag, but his captor only laughed at the sounds coming forth.

"Well my little pet, I'll leave you alone for a while with your thoughts," he said and left.

Baker had never experienced such pain and torments. His entire insides went numb with the cold but at the same time a sensation of fire-like intensity shot through him. He screamed and hollered, twisted and struggled, but nothing he did alleviated the pain searing through him. Tears of agony fear and pain flowed from his eyes. Finally, he simply collapsed in his bondage and prayed to die or get free, but of course neither happened.

CHAPTER SIX: YARD WORK

Somewhere during the time the iced dildo froze Baker's ass and penetrated deep into his prostate, the beleaguered cop passed out. He'd waken periodically but only for a short time, feel the agony of his predicament and pass out again. It took more than a couple of hours for the ice to completely melt but the cop had no idea when that happened. He did not even feel anything when his captor pulled out the now water-bloated condom from his rectum and disposed of it. The cop was beyond knowing or even caring at that stage.

Eventually the man who had captured and tortured him released him from the torturous device he was fastened to and led the semi-conscious cop to the spot on the floor where he had been earlier. The cop was chained once again to steel rings embedded in the cement and left there to sleep. His captor realized that his prisoner could only take so much rough treatment and that he needed to rejuvenate himself. The cop slept fitfully for hours, tossing and turning, mumbling in his sleep and at times even crying out. The jogger enjoyed it all and taped it for watching again in his spare time.

The jogger had set up an elaborate sound system in the building and could hear the cop on speakers in his own room. He sighed contentedly after he had finished his meal and crawled into his bed. The cop was safe where he lay chained and there was no fear of his escaping.

Hours later the jogger, totally refreshed himself, stood over his captive laughing. He took another pitcher of ice cold water and poured it over the cop's head, waking the poor man from his semi-conscious state. It took a few minutes for the cop to once again realize where he was and what had happened. He looked up at the jogger and said, "You bastard, you'll pay for this."

The jogger simply laughed some more.

"Yes my pet, probably in the afterworld, but most likely Satan and I will have a good time laughing about it," the jogger said meanly. "Now, enjoy the water in your bowl, because we have a long, busy day ahead of us."

Despite his wanting to tell his captor to take the water and shove it, the cop was thirsty and knew he needed refreshment, so once again he humiliated himself by lapping up the water in the bowl like some dumb dog. Again, the jogger just laughed. When the cop had finished drinking the jogger led him outside to where the motorcycle was parked. The cop panicked as he thought he was in for another jogging session, but instead the jogger said to him, "Boy, the ride on those country roads with all that dust really dirtied up my new bike. There is a pail of water, some sponges and clothes. I want you to clean my bike until it shines like new. Now get with it."

The cop had no choice and started in cleaning with the water and sponges. Actually, had it not been so demeaning having to clean his own motorcycle like this, he would have enjoyed the task. It was a warm, pleasant day and it felt good to have the sun beating down on him. It took about an hour or so but when he had finished the motorcycle sparkled in that sun. The jogger had sat in a lounge chair nearby, the taser gun in his hand and watched the whole thing, constantly jibing the cop to work faster or pointing out dirty spots he had missed. But when it was done the jogger was obviously pleased.

"Ah yes my little pet, it appears you will indeed make a very good house slave," the jogger chuckled, sounding totally sadistic.

The cop said to himself, "No way you asshole, no fucking way," but kept silent.

"Now my pet, let's see how good you are at yard work," the jogger said, pointing in the direction of the building where he had been holding the cop since capturing him. "Over there, against the wall is a lawnmower."

The cop looked to where the jogger was pointing and saw the old rickety worn out looking mower.

"I want you to cut the grass on my lawn," the jogger went on and the cop looked at him in disbelief. "Sorry to say that my usual gas powered run mower is broken so you'll have to make do with that old-fashioned push type over there. Come along now, get the mower and I'll show you where I want you to cut."

Baker couldn't believe it when his captor showed him the area that needed mowing. It must have been a fifty square yard enclosure. It was full of weeds, twisted plants and even some grass. The poor cop wondered miserably if there was poison ivy in there as well.

"Oh, you may have to pull some of the weeds and other crap before you are able to mow my pet, so you best get started," the jogger said as the cop stood next to him behind the old-fashioned lawnmower he had rolled along with him when the jogger brought him to where he was to do the chore. "I want this done before tonight..."

The cop eyed the taser gun in the jogger's hand, sighed, and set to work. It was backbreaking, sweaty work, made all the more difficult by the fact that his wrists were still handcuffed in front of him. The sun, which had seemed so warm and pleasant on his skin while he had washed the motorcycle, now, was straight up. It was beating down on him unmercifully as he knelt on the ground, pulling weeds and removing stones and debris from the huge patch. His captor had not even given him protective gardening gloves to wear while he did the work. It took him hours of effort with no let-up...the jogger did not allow him to slow down or to even rest, but eventually it was done to the jogger's satisfaction.

CHAPTER SEVEN: DINNER

The cop, exhausted from the strenuous yard work that his captor had forced him to do offered no resistance when he was made to sit back in the "torture chair" (as he had come to call it) and be tied down. He actually was amazed at how deft his captor was at binding him so damned tightly to the chair- his arms crossed against his chest, the wiry-like rope taut against his muscular limbs, legs and chest and his ankles tied off to the legs of the chair...and the rope looped just tight enough around his neck and lashed to the back of the chair to keep him from moving without strangling himself. Although at times he thought it might be better to do just that and end this misery and torture that he was being put through. And why??? WHY??? He wondered. What does this maniac want? Why is he doing this to me; what is he after? Can I somehow escape? These were the questions running through his tortured mind. He knew though that he could not free himself from the bonds of the chair; he had tried before but the ropes were too secure. Plus, the butt-plug wedged in his hole made the sitting in the "torture chair" all the more worse and uncomfortable.

Fuck, but it had been utterly humiliating with the collar around his neck being made to mow the grass, rake it up, move some heavy stones around, all the while sweating in the hot sun. And to make matters worse his captor had sat by, dressed in the cop's uniform, HIS DAMNED UNIFORM, IT WAS HIS, the tall leather boots gleaming, (gleaming because he, the cop had licked them clean, MORTIFYING) the tan pants tight on his muscular legs and constantly laughing at him and calling him degrading names, "my little pet", "killer cop", "boy", "asshole" and worse. But the officer could not fight back because the maniac had the taser ready and aimed…and there was no way Officer Baker was going to risk getting zapped again. When finally he had done the job satisfactorily enough he was brought back into the building… and what a strange building it was…and tied to the chair.

His captor stood over him, smiling that evil smile of his, looking almost adoringly at his captive cop.

"Well, my little pet," he said. "You did a good job. Maybe later I'll let you wash and wax my van and clean out the toilets here, but first I have some errands to do and I'm afraid you cannot accompany me. I do think though that you'll be safe here because even if you were able to get free, which I strongly doubt, there is no way out of this room. You see, I keep it bolt-locked from the outside. So, I'll let you sit here and rest while I'm gone…"

Some rest the cop thought. The bastard had put a handful of ground-up gravel on the seat of the chair before making the cop sit down and tying him to it. Now, besides the butt-plug tormenting his hole, the tiny stones were beginning to cut through the thin material of the jogger's shorts he had on. And they were rubbing against and irritating the fuck out of his already sore ass. If he moved even a little a new stone would find a way to torture him, plus when he moved the butt-plug raped his shit-chute. The little stones irritated him similarly like a stone would do in your shoe when you walked. So all the cop could do was sit there as motionless as possible. Of course it didn't help that the leather blindfold/gag device was once again attached to his face. The maniac constantly bragged about how this was an invention of his own, but all the cop knew was that besides being damned uncomfortable, the fucking thing cut off all light and the leather gag part of the device made speech impossible, except for occasional moans and groans. The officer didn't know how long he sat there this time…hours? Days? It seemed like weeks to him. He was tired and tried to dose off but each time his head would nod he'd feel the rope pulling into his neck and he was jarred back to wakefulness. Instead, he used the time to think of what he would do to his captor once he was able to get free…no way would he bring him to jail, at least not without first getting his own brand of revenge. But the problem of course was getting free. The stones on the chair bit into his reddened and paddled ass cheeks…

Finally, the cop heard the door open and felt the presence of his captor. He had not tried to get free this time for fear of the jogger catching him in the act and paddling his poor ass again. He could not risk another paddling, not for some time.

"Ah," the cop heard. "My little pet is still here, how nice. Well, I have something for you. I'm sure you must be very hungry so I went all the way into town to get you some food. Just give me a few minutes to set up and then you can have your dinner."

Behind his blindfold/gag the cop simply nodded…

Baker hadn't realized until that moment that yes, he was indeed very hungry. Earlier, he had been given some water and some mush-like substance that he was forced to eat out of a bowl on the floor like a dog, but now he was really and truly hungry. He could hear his captor moving around the room, moving chairs and tables and humming softly to himself. And then the captive cop smelled it, the tempting aroma of baked chicken and potatoes. Damn, now he was feeling starved and anxious to get at the food. Finally his captor said that all was ready. He untied the cop from the chair but immediately and roughly cuffed his wrists behind his back. Once the poor cop was secured that way he removed the blindfold/gag. The cop spotted a table set up with a large plate of chicken, some green veggies, and mashed potatoes and on the side a bottle of white wine. It actually looked like a romantic dinner of sorts. The cop headed toward it, but his captor quickly grabbed his upper arm and pulled him back.

"Oh no, no my little pet, not that, that's my dinner," the jogger laughed and then grabbed the cop's other arm as well. "Yours is over here."

And with that he turned the cop around and to the amazement of the cuffed man he saw four articles hanging from a beam by a string each.

"What the fuck?" the cop thought to himself.

"My little pet, I went all the way into town just to get you your favorite food," the captor said directly into the cop's ear as he held his upper arms tight, his lips grazing Baker's lobe as he spoke.

The cop grimaced...

"Everyone knows that cops love donuts so that's what I got you," the jogger said. "I only put four up there but there is a whole dozen waiting in case those aren't enough. And because you worked so hard in my yard I had the bakery make them extra special for you. They're all double filled, one with cream, one with jelly, one lemon and one custard. MMMMM, I'll bet they are delicious."

The cop clenched his teeth as the jogger held him tighter by the arms, pulling him nearly against himself. Now this was not only humiliating, it was inhuman in a way.

"Of course you know that I can't be too easy on you boy," the jogger went on, sounding insanely reasonable somehow. "So I decided that you will have to do this old Halloween trick we did as kids... that is you have to eat each of the donuts as they hang there on the strings. It really should be fun watching you enjoy this meal."

The cop groaned.

"No way," he said. "I'm not going to play that game."

"Ah, but you are my little pet, you are," the jogger said, let go of the cop's arms and suddenly he was pointing the taser at his captive yet again. "You will do it, unless you want to feel the sting of the taser again and then some even worse punishment. And you better eat them all...completely...anything that falls on the floor will have to be eaten too. If you don't do it I'll taser you, punish you and not let you eat till tomorrow evening. Do you understand boy?"

The cop looked at the taser, HIS TASER, in his captor's hand and he knew that he had no choice; besides, he actually was hungry and at least this was better than no food at all. His captor sat down at his table and began on his chicken dinner, ordering the cop to begin on his. The donuts were strung up so they were just a bit higher than the cop's mouth so he had to lift his head up and back to get to them. MORTIFYING! The first one he approached turned out to be the custard filled donut and after the cop had stretched his head and taken a few bights the custard began to ooze out all over his handsome face. He had to work fast to keep it from getting all over him, or worse, from dripping on the floor. He worked diligently at the task but still crumbs and fillings fell to the floor.

His captor sat eating his chicken, drinking his wine and laughing meanly at the cop's efforts.

"Don't worry about what's on the floor boy, you can get that when you've finished all the other donuts," the jogger said from the table. "Now get to it."

And so he did. After the custard came the jelly, then the cream filled and finally the lemon. When he had finished his face, chin, neck and part of his stomach area was covered by a mixed smear of all four fillings.

"Now get what you dropped on the floor and be quick about it boy," the jogger ordered.

The cop dropped to his knees, then, flat on his stomach, and crawled to each pile of crumbs and fillings that had landed on the stone floor. He licked it all up, getting a good supply of dirt and grime along with his meal. His captor, now finished with his own food, laughed and applauded the cop's efforts and prodded him on to any crumb he might have missed. It was great fun for the man and sheer agony for the officer. When he had finished, the cop was allowed to stand. His nemesis faced him and studied the layers of crumbs, filling and dirt on the cop's face.

"Ah, still a lot left here my pet," the jogger said. "Let me help you finish it off."

With that he scraped some of the food off the cop's face with a finger encased in a tight leather glove and made the cop suck, lick and clean it off. This was kept up until the cop's face was relatively clean. Also, the jogger enjoyed the sensations of his fingers being sucked through the leather gloves...and somehow it seemed as if Officer Baker was enjoying sucking those leather gloved fingers... The cop was then led to a corner where a large doggie bowl of water awaited him. He gratefully lay on his stomach and lapped up the water, eager to wash down the doughy meal he had consumed. What Baker didn't know was that his captor had pissed in the bowl earlier so the cop was drinking not just water but his captor's urine as well.

"Well my little pet, you've had quite a day haven't you?" the jogger asked. "Good exercise, a nice quiet rest and a delicious meal. You should be happy."

The cop glared up at him asked, "What the hell have I done to be treated like this?"

The jogger simply laughed.

"Let me go man, let me go," the cop pleaded. "Why are you doing this to me? WHY?"

"Why, my pet?" the jogger asked and stepped close to the cop on the floor. "WHY? Because I can!"

And with that the jogger raised one booted foot, pulled it back and kicked the cop square in the ribs...

"HUUUUHHHFFFFFF!!!!" Baker cried out and curled himself into a fetal position.

Retching and gagging from the pain the cop lay there seething, gasping and crying as the jogger left the room.

CHAPTER EIGHT: SUSPENSION

THWACCCKKKKK went the heavy leather paddle as it connected to the very sore and highly enflamed ass of the captured cop. As his mind returned to the present moment he uttered a "One hundred, thank you Sir" with a defeated sounding sigh. Tears had long since dried on his cheeks. His strength was sapped and he simply stayed where he was- prone on the lap of his captor who was still dressed in a full police uniform, his police uniform.

"Well boy, are you happy with the punishment?" the jogger asked.

"Why are you doing this to me...why?" the cop asked in reply.

"Why boy? You keep asking that," the jogger repeated. "Why? Well, because you are a criminal and criminals need to be punished for their crimes. It is the duty of the police to properly punish all those who disobey the law."

"I'm not a criminal," the captured cop moaned. "I'm a cop, a police officer, I uphold the law."

"BULLSHIT!" the jogger shouted, unnerving the cop over his lap. "You are a criminal. I am the police officer! I am in the police uniform, neatly cleaned, my boots are shiny, and you, you are in ragged jogging clothes, obviously the outfit of a criminal. YOU, you must learn to obey the law."

"No, no, please, I'm a cop," Baker said again, trying to reason with the man. "You can't kidnap and torture a police officer. You'll go to jail for this. Let me go now, please, *please.*"

The man in the police uniform leapt to his feet, causing his captive to fall to the floor.

"DAMN," he shouted. "What the fuck do I have to do to get you to admit to your crimes? You are a criminal, the lowest form of existence. You need to pay for your crimes, to be punished for what you have done!"

The cop saw that this was getting worse; his captor was obviously insane and starting to come apart. But nonetheless he would not give in nor surrender to him...

"I haven't done anything wrong," the muscular but exhausted captive cried out from the stone floor where he had fallen.

But the uniformed man didn't listen; he muttered to himself something about really teaching this asshole once and for all. He went to the nearby cabinet and returned with a huge coil of rope, which he used quickly, methodically and professionally to tie the cop's arms and wrists to his sides, totally securing his victim.

"OH GOD, no, no, what now man???" the cop rasped as he was tied tighter and tighter.

Ignoring his captive yet again the jogger pulled the man up by his ear, evincing a howl-like scream from the victim. He walked the cop to another part of the building where he unceremoniously dumped him back on the floor.

"You are a disgrace, just look at yourself, you're a fucking mess," the jogger ranted.

Of course the captive cop couldn't actually look at himself but he could feel the dirt, grime, sweat and piss which had accumulated over his body and clothes in the last few days.

"Fucking pig," the man continued.

Then, he produced a large knife, which made the tied man tremble when he saw it, thinking he was about to be stabbed, but instead he felt the ragged and torn jogging clothes that he had been forced to don being cut from his body. Soon the clothes were cut off and the victim was totally nude except for the sneakers and sweat socks on his feet. The uniformed captor giggled as he then removed the sneakers and then pulled the sweat stained athletic socks off the cop's feet.

"Such beautiful feet you have my criminal friend," he said. "But oh how these socks do stink. Here, sample how disgusting you are."

With that he took one sock and stuffed it into his victim's mouth.

"Taste good my little criminal?" he asked the cop snidely.

Using more rope the captor tightly lashed the victim's ankles together, then just under and above his knees. The poor victim was totally immobilized. He closed his eyes, trying hard not to gag and retch on the foul tasting filthy sock stuffed in his mouth. And because of that he didn't see the large metal hook that his captor attached to the heavy strands of rope which tied his ankles together.

"Now my criminal thug, one more time, do you admit that you have committed many, many crimes and that you must pay for them?" the jogger asked the cop.

All the victimized cop could do was mumble a "No" through his sock gag. The captor giggled again, stepped over to a sort of control panel on the wall of the room they were in and opened it. He pulled a switch and suddenly the cop's eyes flared open… Baker was astonished to find himself being dragged across the floor a little bit and then lifted by his tied and hooked feet into the air.

"RRRRHHHHHMMMFFFF!!!!" he screamed around the sock in his mouth.

He pleaded with his wide open eyes for his captor to let him down, but of course that was not to be. Finally, his face was even with the face of his captor, six feet off the floor. The cop swayed in the air, twisting his body, trying desperately to raise his chest and head up, but he couldn't maintain the position. He watched as his captor opened a three foot square opening in the floor just below him and lit a fire in what turned out to be a gas burner type device. The swinging victim looked down in sheer horror.

The smelly sock was removed from the cop's mouth and dropped on the flame, immediately catching fire and burning. The victim screamed, "What the fuck are you doing??? LET ME DOWN! DAMN YOU MAN!!"

"Ah my little criminal friend, let me explain," the jogger said with a grin. "See that large bladder-like contraption over there?"

The cop strained his neck to see where the jogger was gesturing toward. He saw the device the man was referring to.

"That device is filled with water and it acts as a counterbalance to the weight of your body," the man explained to the terrified cop. "As long as the water level stays the same you will remain in the position you are currently in. But, should the water leak out then the bladder will go up and you, you my pretty thug will go down. Down doesn't necessarily lead to hell but it's still very hot down there. Now, do you admit that you are a criminal and have committed so many crimes that you have to pay for?"

"NO, NO, YOU'RE NUTS! I'M A COP! I'M A GODDAMNED COP AND A GOOD ONE AT THAT! YOU'RE THE CRIMINAL," the cop screeched crazily. "DAMN YOU LET ME DOWN!"

"Well, I guess you give me no choice," the jogger said.

The swinging upside down cop watched in horror and total fear as his captor stepped over to the bladder device and turned on a small faucet near the bottom of it. At once water started trickling out, not in a big gush, but a slow, steady stream. The swinging man struggled even harder, finding renewed strength, but very slowly he felt himself dropping and felt, or imagined, the heat of the fire below.

"Now then, are you ready to confess to your crimes?" the jogger asked the cop again. "Tell Officer Baker all about them."

"NO, NO, I'M OFFICER BAKER, YOU'RE THE CRIMINAL," the cop screamed louder yet. "OH GOD, STOP THIS PLEASE!!!"

The more he squirmed and twisted the faster the water poured from the tap.

"That fire is hot enough now," the jogger mused. "It'll probably burn the hair off your head ala Michael Jackson, and then maybe a lot of skin from your handsome face. So just confess to me. I am Officer Baker and you are a criminal."

"NO, NO, PLEASE!" the cop wailed as he hung there. "DON'T DO THIS! YOU'RE CRAZY!"

"Crazy?" the jogger asked. "No, I am Officer Baker. Confess to being a criminal and maybe I can find some leniency for you, despite all your crimes."

The victim had stopped trying to swing away from the fire but he felt the heat closer and closer to his head. He didn't see his captor toss the other dirty sock on the fire, but he felt the heat as it flared up.

"OH SHIT...PLEASE DON'T DO THIS...PLEASE...PLEASE...PLEASE DON'T ROAST ME ALIVE...PLEASE...OFFICER BAKER!" the cop pleaded.

"Ah, now we are getting somewhere," the jogger said happily, looking at the sweat and tear soaked face of the man as he hung like a side of beef. "So you admit that it is I who is Officer Baker?"

"Yes, yes, you are Officer Baker, Police Officer Baker," the cop cried, wondering who was saying the words he was hearing coming from his mouth.

"And you, do you confess to being a criminal?" the jogger asked, reached over and pushed the sweating hanging man, sending him swinging back and forth like a pendulum.

When the victim stopped swinging his head was less than fifteen inches from the fire. He was sweaty and his face was bloated looking at that point. He could feel the heat of it against his moist skin.

"Yes Officer Baker, I confess, I am a criminal," Baker shouted. "And I deserve to be punished."

"Then you will sign a confession admitting to all the crimes you have committed?" the jogger asked.

"Yes Officer Baker, whatever you want," the cop replied through trembling and now puffed up lips. "I'll sign anything Officer. I am a criminal."

He realized he was starting to be cooked…

With that the new Officer Baker turned off the faucet, stopping the flow of the water and with brute strength lifted the newly admitted criminal away from the fire. He lowered the criminal to the floor and untied the ropes from his ankles and legs. He had to lift the trembling and sweated victim to his feet and actually hold him while he led him to still another area of the building. The cop was crying profusely and thanking his captor at the same time, blubbering out his words.

"We can do the written confession later, now you must start your jail term," the jogger said. "All criminals must have a jail cell. And here is yours. It isn't too big but you don't have to worry about cell mates. In jail white boys like you can be easy victims to more experienced criminal types, so it's probably better that you have your own cell, at least for now."

The cop looked at the small enclosure he was about to be deposited in and the jogger went on with his speech.

"It doesn't have a bed but there is an old lumpy mattress on the floor and that should be good enough for a thug like you," the jogger said, pointing at the mattress. "Also, there is a hole in one corner which you can use as your toilet. Notice that the door is solid steel and that it has a small window in which I can look into to see that you are obeying the rules. But I keep the window blocked by a sliding steel panel when I'm not around. Don't worry Criminal, you'll get used to the dark in time."

The newly admitted criminal simply sighed, too exhausted, too beaten and too heat stricken to argue.

"And you will no longer use your name," the jogger continued, holding the cop's upper arm tight as they stood in front of the cell. "From now on you will be nothing but a number. You are prisoner two four six zero one. You will answer to that number at all times. And you will stand at attention whenever I approach and you will say, prisoner two four six zero one ready for inspection Officer Baker SIR. Is that understood?"

"Yes Officer Baker, SIR," the cop said softly, stood himself at attention and his shriveled cock started to stiffen a bit. "Thank you Officer..."

"Good prisoner two four six zero one," the jogger said and let go of the cop's arm. "Now, I think it is probably best to keep your arms and hands tied to your sides for now, until you become accustomed to your role. Now, get into your cell prisoner two four six zero one."

Prisoner two four six zero one did as he was told and stepped slowly into the cell. He collapsed on the thin, small mattress on the cold stone floor, unable to do much with his arms still tightly tied. And he cried...he cried loud sobbing tears.

The new Officer Baker listened outside the door and smiled to himself. His revenge was taking shape.

CHAPTER NINE: THE CONFESSION AND THE TRUTH

Both the captor and the captive slept soundly that night, their roles totally reversed; the cop was now the jogger and the captor/ jogger had become the cop. The jogger awoke and turned on the monitor from the hidden infrared cameras in his prisoner's cell. He saw that the prisoner still slept on the thin mattress, his muscular arms tightly tied to his sides, the bondage making him look all the more sexy. He tossed and turned and occasionally moaned and the captor was happy to hear the man mutter things in his sleep like, "not a cop… "Prisoner two four six zero one…" "…taser gun, obey" and the man felt confident that he had indeed succeeded in breaking down the once haughty cop. The cop would now be easy to control and manipulate from now on.

After a hearty breakfast and a warm shower the captor went to the prisoner's cell and opened the door.

"Wake up prisoner!" he yelled, and then poured some ice cold water on the prone figure.

The former cop awoke, stunned, confused and tried to move but with his arms lashed to his sides this wasn't easy. He looked up at the imposing figure of the man in the police uniform and then he struggled to his knees. Finally, he managed to stand up at attention and said, "Prisoner two four six zero one ready for inspection Officer Baker SIR." The captor smiled with sadistic pleasure.

"Good boy," he said. "Now, come with me…"

The prisoner was led to another part of the building and the ropes were removed from his arms.

"Its time we cleaned you up two four six zero one," the jogger said, handing the former cop a bar of soap. "Here's some soap. Go in the shower stall there and clean yourself thoroughly. I do not want to be able to smell you the way you smell now."

With a blank look on his face the prisoner did as he was told and stepped into the open shower. The jogger had kept the taser gun at the ready, concealed, but at the ready, just in case the cop was faking his performance. He knew that untying him completely was really taking a large chance. When the former cop turned on the water and felt it pouring down over his head and cascading over his body he couldn't have been happier. He used the soap to clean the dirt, muck, piss, grime and sweat of three days from his body and it made him feel like a new man when he stepped from the shower and stood before his MASTER.

"Thank you Officer Baker for this honor SIR," he said and actually meant it.

The jogger was in seventh heaven…

The former cop felt so thankful for the man standing there in the police uniform that he would have done anything the man asked. After he dried himself off with towels provided by his captor the prisoner was led to another room where he was handed an orange jump suit, the type all jail prisoners wear. It was a little tight over his muscular body but it obviously gave his captor pleasure seeing him in it, so he again thanked Officer Baker for the gift.

"Now two four six zero one, you still look a little ragged," the jogger said, truly enjoying himself now. "We need to shave you. Sit here on this stool and I'll get the shaving gear.'

The jogger again kept the taser gun at the ready, seeing as not only was the cop not restrained in any way at the moment, but he was actually leaving him alone and unfettered this time. It was a good test to see if the cop had really been broken down. The prisoner sat staring blankly forward and soon the officer was back with scissors, shaving cream, hot steaming water in a large basin and a razor. All this he wheeled in a small trolley-like device. He first used towels soaked in the hot water to soften the skin on the prisoner's face. Not once did the former cop protest about the towels being too hot or irritating his skin. He simply sat there as the jogger worked on him barber style. The jogger then lathered up the prisoner's face with mounds of shaving cream, let the lather soak in and then deftly whisked it off with the razor. As he shaved the prisoner's neck area he held the former cop's face upward with two fingers squeezing his nose. Again the prisoner did not protest as he was worked on. Actually, the prisoner couldn't believe how fresh and revived being shaved made him feel and he again thanked his MASTER, thanking him profusely.

"Ah, but it's not complete," the man said. "We should get rid of that uncomely looking hair on your head. Hold still while I take care of that problem as well two four six zero one."

The prisoner was a tad taken aback at the thought of having his head shaved, but he thought that if it pleased his MASTER to remove the hair then that was all that mattered. In short order, using the scissors, more hot towels, more lather and the razor the prisoner's head was soon as bare and shiny as a cue ball. The MASTER held up a hand mirror to show the prisoner who was stunned at how different he looked from when he was a…but he couldn't really remember what he had looked like before or what he had been before. The only thing that mattered now was that his MASTER wanted him to look this way and so he was happy to be bald. Again he professed his sincere thanks to the captor for what he had done.

The prisoner was ordered to follow his new MASTER to still another room in the building and he was surprised to see a table set up with food on it.

"You must eat two four six zero one because I don't want you to waste away and be unable to work," the jogger explained. "Since you are a prisoner and a slave obviously you are not allowed to sit at a table. But I've prepared a plate of food for you and it's on the floor, where you will always eat your meals. Also, there are glasses of orange juice and milk and a cup of coffee there. In the future you will always eat without the use of your hands, but since this is your first full meal this is one time I will allow you to use them and a knife and fork. Now, on your knees and eat while the food is still warm."

As the prisoner did as he was told and reached for the knife the jogger held the taser at the ready…

The prisoner could not believe how lucky he was as he gratefully ate all that was put on his metal plate. Without a doubt, he told himself, that this was the greatest meal he had ever had in his life. His captor sat at the table drinking coffee watching his new slave and enjoying the sight. Yes, he thought, two four six zero one is a fine, fine specimen and that tight jumpsuit really emphasizes his physique. I think that boy is going to bring me months and months and then years of sexual pleasure.

When both MASTER and slave had finished their meals two four six zero one was made to pick up all the dishes and clean them in a sink. Then, he was told that he was always to walk a foot to the side and two steps behind the MASTER whenever they moved. The slave understood the order immediately and happily fell into step as they went to yet another room in the building. The prisoner was surprised to see that this room contained a large double-sized bed and he was even more surprised when his MASTER ordered him to strip off the jumpsuit and get on the bed. He did as ordered and then watched as the MASTER himself stripped. The prisoner was equally surprised and awed at the MASTER'S sleek, muscular build, his thick muscular thighs and abs. The MASTER climbed on the bed with the prisoner/slave and began slowly to gently rub his hands over his prize, the taser gun very nearby in case the former cop decided he did not want to be handled. However, two four six zero one found himself becoming aroused as his MASTER played with his body and soon found himself responding by lapping and sucking on his MASTER'S nips. The two men were soon wrapped up in each other, arms and legs entangled and intermeshed. The MASTER started kissing the slave, letting his tongue go deep into the prisoner's mouth and to the surprise of the slave he found it to be exciting.

The MASTER deftly maneuvered his slave's mouth down his body toward his crotch and the slave, as if he had been born to do this soon had the man's cock in his mouth as he licked, lapped and sucked on it. The cock grew to over nine thick inches and although the prisoner gagged a little he had no real problem in taking it all in. Soon the MASTER was face-fucking his now owned boy but when the pre-cum began to ooze out the MASTER expertly flipped his willing partner over and thrust his throbbing cock into the boy's shit hole. At first the prisoner let out a cry of pain and shock and the jogger quickly looked to where he had the taser. He wanted to be ready in case Officer Baker returned. But then, amazingly as his MASTER systematically and rhythmically fucked him he experienced a feeling of fulfillment, a joy, an excitement, a thrill like none other he had ever known. He sensed his MASTER tensing up and then felt a warm flow erupt inside him. He heard his MASTER sigh and then felt him gently collapse on his body. The two lay there for a few minutes, both exhausted. Then the MASTER rolled off his slave, turned the prisoner over and noted a huge erection on the boy. The MASTER lowered his own lips over the erection and with amazingly little effort on his part sucked the cum from the prisoner's cock.

After a while the two men lying on the bed, their bodies intertwined in each other, the MASTER looked at his slave and said, "Well two four six zero one, did you enjoy that?"

"Oh yes Officer Baker, yes, thank you," the slave replied happily. "I've never felt anything like that before."

The captor caressed the former cop's chin as he said, "You are mine now boy. You belong to me. You are my slave, my prisoner.

You will work and take what I dish out on you on a daily basis to make up for the wrong and evil you did when you were a cop."

"But Officer Baker, MASTER, please, what did I do to displease you?" the slave asked, sounding totally bewildered.

"I had a lover, a boy I would have done anything for, he was my entire life," the jogger began, finally revealing why he had done what he did in abducting Officer Baker. "He was a good boy, maybe naïve but honest and good. I had to leave on a business trip to Europe and was gone for almost two months. When I got back I learned that my lover had died, killed himself actually. He was in jail and apparently some of the other prisoners worked him over badly and he couldn't take it and thought that death was better than a long term in prison."

"MASTER, what was he in prison for?" the slave asked, still sounding confused.

"You should know the answer to that boy," the MASTER replied. "You arrested him on some false charge and you must have planted crack on him. I know my boy and he never used drugs or had anything whatsoever to do with them, so I know he didn't have any on him when he was arrested. Since I wasn't there to post bail he was placed in jail until his trial, but he never made it. I have friends in certain places and got them to provide me with the police reports. Your name is listed as the arresting officer. So you see I have to make you pay for what you did."

"But MASTER, it couldn't have been me," the slave responded. "I'm a motorcycle, traffic cop; I don't work drugs or criminal activities in the department. I just do traffic. I could not have been the officer who arrested your lover, honest MASTER."

The former jogger was stunned because he knew that the slave had just spoken the truth. He had made a mistake, an awful mistake. He had kidnapped and tortured the wrong man. Meanwhile a bent and twisted cop was still out there, probably still pulling the same tricks. The captor was torn at what he had done, taken this beautiful young cop prisoner and broken him down to the obedient slave now laying there beside him. Well, it was too late now, there was nothing he could do to change or undo what had been done and what had happened. At least two four zero six one seemed happy being there, as he clung tightly to his MASTER'S body.

EPILOGUE

A few weeks later Sergeant Robert Barker of the city's gang unit and his new partner had just stopped and cuffed a young punk. They were ready to take him in. Barker took a couple of small cellophane packets from his jacket pocket, put them in the prisoner's pocket and then took them out again.

"Well, well, look here," Sergeant Barker said. "This punk was carrying crack on him. This should be enough to put him away for a long, long time."

The punk started to protest and Barker smacked him hard across the face with his leather gloved hand.

"Shut-up asshole, you're in enough trouble already," Barker rasped at the terrified young guy. "So don't go piss me off anymore."

Barker's partner took the sergeant aside and questioned what had just happened. The cocky sergeant replied, "Fuck 'em, doesn't matter if he was or wasn't carrying this time. He probably did before and will again. We're just putting an end to his criminal life now. Good riddance to fucking trash like him. And don't worry, I've done this before and no one questioned it."

Unnoticed in a darkened doorway a short distance away, a shadowy figure, dressed as a jogger, watched and listened to this exchange. It was too bad that Sergeant Barker couldn't see the grin on the jogger's face.

AND YET ANOTHER NIGHT TRAPPED AT THE LOCAL

As told by: Greg Smith, from his journal
Written by: Christopher Trevor

Saturday night and I had nothing to do. That's pretty sad and pathetic for a young single and reasonably handsome guy like me. What I really wanted to do was go to the Local, wash down a few cold beers, maybe meet a hot number and bring the stud home for some real sweaty and sexy good times. And I didn't mean a stud that would tie me the fuck up and work me over, but someone who would treat me right for a change. Not that there's anything wrong with getting tied up and worked over, if that's your thing, just that I'd had enough of that lately to last me a lifetime…and seeing as I tended to meet the wrong guys who would tie me up and work me over I really wanted some vanilla loving for a change. But truthfully, I was too apprehensive about going to the Local. I mean, most guys would be if they were me. It seemed that lately every time I went to the sleazy bar those two clowns who owned the place, Alex and Ronald got the jump on me and roped me the fuck up in that bathroom stall. As I've said before, you know the stall, the one with the infamous glory hole carved in the door of it. Too many times I had been forcibly stripped to my goddamned socks and roped up in there with my poor cock and juicy balls sticking out of the glory hole for all to get at and suck and torture any way they wanted to. I had actually lost count of how many times I had been more than milked dry in there, how many guys had had at my big meaty cock. Fuck, some of them even went so far as to climb up into the stall behind me and fuck my hole a few times each, if they could get it up that many times, getting their jollies squeezing my big nipples as well while in there fucking the very tar out of me. Most times those two bastards Alex and Ronald blindfolded me for the duration that I was tied to the stall door so there really was no way to identify who had been in the stall fucking me. Shit, I couldn't even prove to the cops that Alex and Ronald *had forcibly* put me in that stall and roped me up like a caught steer. It was their word against mine after all. (Fuck, I had even heard it told that a few of the guys who had sucked me off and fucked me rear-wise were cops…) And none of the patrons of the bar would admit to finding some poor guy all roped up in a bathroom stall of all places. Shit, if they admitted to it that would be the end of their kinky and twisted fun. And how many pairs of underpants had I lost to Alex after being roped up in that stall? I did not know anymore. The fucking guy loves keeping my damned shorts as souvenirs of his and Ronald's conquests of me. As I sat there in my living room not really watching the TV that was on I became more and more restless…and more and more horned up as well. That decided it I thought angrily. I *would not* allow anyone to intimidate me or to frighten me out of having a good time and enjoying myself. God knows I spent enough time being frightened recently when Leo had me in his clutches, but that's a story for another time, definitely another time. I stood up and walked with purpose to my bedroom to get changed and spiffed up for what *I decided* would be a great yet uneventful night at the Local. About ten minutes later I was dressed in a light green suit, a crisp white shirt, a silk patterned tie and black wingtips with black calf length nylon socks. Looking real good I thought to myself with a grin. I came out of the bedroom and decided that when I had to use the men's room at the Local I would be sure, doubly sure actually, that there were a few other men in there too. Alex and Ronald would not dare to try anything on me in a crowded men's room. Sadly for me though I would find out otherwise…

I walked the short distance to the Local and about a half hour later at nine-thirty PM I walked into the place. My heart was thundering fiercely in my chest. So much for not feeling intimidated huh? The bar was smoke filled and sort of crowded. That was good. I made my way over to the bar and found a stool that afforded me a good view of the men's room. I sat down and glanced over at the men's room. I saw a few guys come out and a couple more go in.

"What'll it be handsome guy?" the bartender asked me.

"Oh," I said, turning to face him. "Uh, I'll have a Budweiser on tap, large please, thanks."

He was tall with dark short cut hair, big blue eyes and his biceps that were sticking out of the rolled up sleeves of his white tee shirt attested to the fact, that like me, he worked out on a regular basis.

"Coming right up," the bartender said to me, placing a frosted mug in front of me and filling it to the rim with beer from the bar tap.

"There you go, that'll be five bucks," he said.

"Thanks," I replied and placed a five dollar bill on the bar along with a couple of singles.

"Thank you," he then replied politely.

As I sipped my beer the bartender looked at me quizzically yet lustfully.

"Something wrong?" I asked him politely.

"No, just that I recall the last time you were here you came in wearing a suit and tie," he said to me, reaching forward and giving my tie a fast tug. "A handsome guy like you in a suit and tie really brings some class to this dump."

I smiled at him, took another sip of my beer and placed the mug down on the bar.

"Tell you what," he said, pulling me close to him by my tie and placing a hand on the back of my neck as well.

He whispered in my ear, "Next beer is on me, just don't say anything."

"Okay," I responded happily and he gave my earlobe a fast lick.

My cock pounded and was hard in my suit pants as he let go of my neck. Who said that wearing something spiffy to a sleaze bar was a waste of time? The bartender smiled at me and went off to serve other patrons. I felt that it was going to be a good night at the Local after all. I lifted my feet off the floor and placed them on the rungs of the stool I was sitting on. The sounds of old disco music filled the smoky bar as I sipped my beer and noshed on pretzels that were in a bowl in front of me and the guy seated next to me at the bar.

When I was halfway through with my first beer the bartender placed a second one in front of me. We nodded knowingly at each other. I chugged down the rest of my first beer and placed the empty mug down in front of me. I sipped my second beer and saw that the place was starting to really crowd up. When the bartender got a break he came over to me and leaned on the bar, his face very close to mine.

"What's your name handsome guy?" he asked me.

"I'm Greg," I replied, holding out my hand.

"I'm Pete," he said and shook my hand tightly. "It's nice to meet you Greg."

He pumped my hand, looking at me lustfully again.

"As I said a handsome guy like you in a suit and tie really dresses this place up," Pete said to me, still holding onto my hand.

"Thank you again, and for the beer," I replied.

"So, what are you doing later tonight?" Pete asked me. "I'm really not supposed to hit on the customers but in your case I really can't help myself."

I smiled, feeling myself blush and said, "Nothing that I know of at the moment."

"That's good Greg," Pete said, still holding my hand in his. "I get off when this dump closes at four AM, if you come back at that time I'd love to treat you to an early breakfast, or maybe a very late dinner…your choice handsome guy."

I smiled even more-so, jokingly told Pete that I would not tell the owners of the dump known as The Local that he had hit on me and gratefully accepted his invitation to a very late dinner.

"I didn't plan to stay here till four AM, but I don't live too far away…" I began.

"I'll come to your place and pick you up Greg, it would be my pleasure," he said, sounding almost pleading. "But you have to promise me one thing."

"And what's that?" I asked as he let go of my hand and playfully straightened my tie for me.

"Please wear your suit and tie; you look so beautiful in it…" Pete said.

"Deal," I responded and quickly jotted down my home address for him. He took the paper that I had written on and slid it down the front section of his jeans, looking at me lustfully again as he did so. I smiled from ear to ear, my cock hard and throbbing in my suit pants. I wondered if I would be able to wait till four AM for this man. Pete pecked me on the lips and said that he had to get back to work. I watched as he sauntered off to serve more patrons. Halfway through my second beer I was feeling very relaxed and mellow, partly thanks to the beers and mostly thanks to the handsome bartender named Pete. It really had turned out to be a good night after all. And best of all, not a sign of Alex or Ronald anywhere. I figured they had taken the night off...

When I was done with my second beer I was feeling totally relaxed. It was a wonderful mellow relaxed sort of feeling. I smiled over at Pete as he served a patron seated a few stools down from me. Besides feeling relaxed however, I was also feeling that I had to use the bathroom. To state it plainly I had to piss pretty badly. I glanced over at the men's room door and saw two men walk through it and into the bathroom. That was just the cue I needed. I stood up, saw that Pete was busy with more customers, and not wanting to bother him I walked quickly through the crowded bar to the men's room. The two guys that I had seen go in there were standing at a urinal each with their backs to me. I saw that one of the stall doors was closed as well. Perfect, I was not alone in the men's room this time. I stood at the urinal between the two men and unzipped my pants. Relief filled me as I pissed like crazy into the urinal. As I was pissing pretty heavily the two men finished their business and walked out of the men's room. Seeing as I was pissing like a racehorse (as the saying goes that we used to use in the military) I could not just bolt out of there. Besides, whoever was in the stall was in the men's room as well. I was still not alone in there. When I finally finished pissing I packed my cock back into my suit pants, turned around, and headed for the door of the men's room. Suddenly, the door to the men's room swung open and I was face to fucking face with Alex.

"Well, well, good evening Socks ol' boy, haven't seen you here lately, since the other night that is," Alex said laughingly as the door to the men's room closed behind him.

"Alex, get out of my way," I said, standing in front of the occupied stall and pointing back at it with a shaking finger. "If you try anything this time I will have a witness."

Alex smirked and then the stall door I was standing in front of opened. Ronald stepped out of the stall and stood there looking at me hungrily.

"*Shit,*" I whispered.

"Snagged again huh Socks ol' boy?" Alex taunted me.

"We'll see about that," I said through clenched teeth.

As I was about to push past Alex Ronald reached out and grabbed me by my arm. He forcefully yanked me back and against himself. Holding me tight by my upper arms the big galloot clamped his mouth down on mine, hard.

"RRRRMMMMFFFFFF!!!" I sputtered angrily as Ronald's tongue explored my mouth.

He darted his tongue against mine, sucked my tongue between his mangy lips and then kissed me and kissed me and kissed me, his lips pressing so hard against mine that I found it hard to pull away. Our tongues crashed against each other in my mouth, vying for space it seemed. The way he was kissing me it felt as if he was trying to snake his goddamned tongue down my throat.

"HHHRRRRMMFFF!!!" I wailed miserably, feeling like I was about to start choking.

When the big guy stopped kissing me he let go of me and I stood there straightening out my suit jacket, catching my breath at the same time.

"Bastard," I muttered.

"I've always wanted to know what those lips of yours tasted like Big guy," Ronald said, smacking his lips with his tongue.

"Well, now that you know I'll be on my way," I said miserably, wanting to get back out to the bar and see Pete again.

"Uh, not so fast Socks," Alex said, now standing in front of the stall with the glory hole carved into its front door.

He pushed the stall door open and piled on the closed toilet was mounds and mounds of rope.

"You have a date Socks," Alex chirped merrily. "I do hope those balls of yours are chock filled with your sticky and sweet nectar."

"And if they're not we got Viagra and powerful vitamin supplements for you Big guy," Ronald added, holding up a pill bottle and quickly putting it back in his pocket.

"HA, after the first two hours or so of him being sucked off we'll feed him a few of those," Alex said to Ronald. "I have no doubt that more than a few guys will want at that big steely cock of his. And we'll want him good and stacked up and shooting loads till at least just before closing time."

"No, no, not this shit again," I muttered angrily as the two men taunted me meanly, backing away from Alex and the stall. "I'm not some bull on a farm that you can just milk and siphon for the fucking fuck of it."

From behind Ronald grabbed me by my upper arms again in a tight vise-like grip.

"UHHHHHFFFFF!!!" I gasped as I struggled in his grasp and he hoisted me a few inches off the floor, the tips of my wingtips dancing against the floor. "Been working out huh you mindless fuck?"

As I struggled Ronald half dragged half carried me over to where Alex was standing at the stall door.

"FUCKER, let go of me man," I ranted and spat angrily.

"Here he is Alex," Ronald said. "Let's get him stripped to his socks and roped up in that stall. I can't fucking wait to suck and slurp a few hearty loads out of him."

"Neither can some of our customers out there," Alex responded and reached for my necktie.

"Shit, shit, *shit!!!*" I rasped as Alex slowly and sexily undid my tie and then slid it off me.

A few moments later I was blindfolded with my tie as the two men held me by my arms and spun me round and round and round, dizzying me, making me disoriented, dancing me stupidly on my wingtips.

"UUUUUUUHHHHH...sons of bitches, stop this, STOP THIS," I panted as my head and my whole body was spun like a top.

The laughed meanly as they spun me what must have been at least fifty times clockwise and then set me round counter-clockwise. When they started spinning me clockwise again I could no longer feel the floor beneath my feet. I heard them laughing and later realized why. They had let go of me and yet I continued spinning myself round and round, I was that disoriented at that point...just as the two jokesters wanted me so that stripping me would be all that much easier.

"Fucking bastards, is this any way to be treating a customer?" I seethed and after they stopped spinning me and balanced me somewhat I felt my suit jacket being taken off me.

Being that I was pretty mellowed from the beers I had drunk and totally dizzied from being spun like a top I really couldn't do all that much to stop the two clowns from stripping me. Ronald held my arms tight, keeping me balanced as Alex did the honors of slowly unbuttoning my white dress shirt. In seconds it was pulled off me, no tee shirt underneath. I stood there with my muscular chest bared, totally on display, for the entire world to see...

"Oh fuck yes Socks ol' boy," Alex mused and I felt his mouth close on one of my big nipples.

"OHHHHHHHHH..." I moaned in forced ecstasy as the guy clipped my tit between his front-most teeth, teased it with his tongue-tip and sucked it hard.

In my already dizzied state my head spun even more as I was held in place and one of my tits was sucked like a lollipop. My cock grew stiffer yet in my suit pants...fuck it all, but I am a sucker for having my tits sucked and slurped and eaten and mashed and tweaked and just all out worked on...

As Alex sucked one of my nipples he twirled my other one with the tips of his thumb and first finger.

"UUUUUUHHHHHH..." I moaned again, feeling as if my cock would burst right through the fabric of my underpants and suit slacks. "FUCKERS, this shit is against the law, you can't do this to a paying customer... got to admit though that feels great..."

The two men snickered and when Alex stopped playing my tits like they were a musical instrument he was tuning Ronald's grip on my arms grew tighter yet. I felt Alex undoing the buckle of my belt and then the clasp on my suit pants.

"NO, NO, oh God no!!!!" I ranted through clenched teeth and Ronald yanked my arms behind me at that point.

I felt beyond powerless, beyond humiliated and beyond angry at myself for having come to the Local. When oh the fuck when would I ever learn? As my suit pants slid down my legs and pooled around my ankles I thought of Pete the bartender. The guy had asked that I wear my suit when he took me out for a late dinner that night. As I felt my suit pants being taken off me over my shoes and socks I wondered if I would make my date with Pete...fuck I wondered if I would still have my suit when the night was over...

As the two men laughed more and more my shoes were unlaced and popped off my feet. Down and off came my white briefs and into Alex's pocket I was sure they went...even blindfolded I didn't need three guesses to know that for sure...as I mentioned the guy loves keeping my damned under shorts as souvenirs of his and Ronald's conquests of me... My cock betrayed me by being hard as concrete between my legs and my balls dangled down real low, chock filled, as Alex had put it with my sticky and sweet nectar...

A few moments later I was standing there clad in just my damned black calf length socks and my necktie turned blindfold. Alex was again sucking and slurping one of my nipples, tweaking and twisting the other one while Ronald did the chore of getting my wrists bound behind me... As one of my nipples was sucked and slurped and the other twisted and tweaked my cock twitched long and hard between my muscular legs. I was all beefed up and pre cum dribbled from my wide sexy slit.

"I think he's just about ready," I heard Ronald say as he finished binding my hands tightly behind me.

"BASTARDS, if you guys know what's good for you you'll let me get dressed and get out of here," I swore on their deaf ears.

When Alex stopped working my nipples a short while later I found myself standing pressed up against the door of the stall. From behind me I imagined it was Alex guiding my big stork of a fear hard cock and my big juicy balls through the infamous glory hole carved in the front of the stall door.

"RRRRRRRRR..." I roared as I was handled in my most private of areas.

Outside the stall I felt a liberal amount of rope being wound around and around the base of my cock and balls and then knotted off tightly, thus preventing me from pulling my pride and joy back into the stall after I'd shot my load.

"The way his cock and balls are tied up out here will keep him hard for a while after he shoots a load or a few," Ronald said as Alex got busy behind me looping rope over and over my upper body and around the stall door, binding me to the structure.

"Good idea again," Alex replied as Ronald did his part roping me up outside the stall door, assisting Alex as he fed the rope through the slots at the side of the sides of the stall.

Once my upper body was securely bound to the stall door I felt another length of rope being wound around and around my black socked ankles. Being blindfolded I had no idea who it was tying up my damned feet, making me totally immobile now in the stall, no chance of getting out of that bathroom. My cock pounded thick, veiny and fear-hard in the glory hole.

"There we go, all nice and packaged for the night," Alex quipped from behind me, giving my melon shaped ass cheeks a tight squeeze each.

"You fucking lowlife bastards," I seethed from my bound up position, feeling totally violated and humiliated. "What's the point of all this???"

"Just making our clientele all the more happy Socks ol' Socks," Alex said and swatted me hard across my ass cheeks with his wide open palm.

"OUUUCCHHH!!!" I yelled miserably. "Oh yeah? Well let me tell you, you smart ass, this time you've got a certain employee out there who just may not like the idea of what you two have done to me here again and…OHHHHHHHHHHHHH…"

Suddenly, my words were cut short as, from outside the stall, Ronald slurped my hard throbbing boner into his greedy mouth. He began sucking me for what felt like all he was worth.

"OHHHHHHHH...fucking guy Ronald loves being the first to get me off..." I snarled through clenched teeth.

"Oh? And just who might that employee be Socks?" Alex chuckled from behind me, and as he spoke I felt him slide his own steely boner between the cheeks of my ass, penetrating me deep and hard.

"AWWWWWWW!!!!" I roared at the painful invasion with no lube on it.

I realized my mistake and clamped my mouth shut, no way would I get Pete in trouble or be the reason he could risk losing his job...

Then, the sounds of my cock being sucked outside the stall and the sounds of dry thrusts in and out of my asshole inside the stall filled the men's room...

Being that I had not shot a load in a few days I came pretty quickly, grunting like a real slob as I filled Ronald's craw with my mess and he gulped it down like a madman.

"AAAARRRRHHHHHYEAH, fucking A, bastards," I rasped breathlessly as I shot my load and then at the same time Alex shot his load in my hole, warming up my shit chute with his juices.

"OOOOOOOOOOOO...SOCKS, yeah," Alex crooned from behind me, his steel hard cock still filling my hole as he seemed to cum and cum alongside me as I filled Ronald's craw myself.

"FUCK, FUCK, what a scene this is," I moaned and then I felt Alex's cock deflate a bit and it slipped and slid slowly from my crevice.

Alex leaned against me from behind and kissed my big curled biceps a few times before he packed himself back into his pants and I heard him zip up...

"Fucking bastards," I whispered, my forehead pressed against the stall door as I heard Alex climbing out of the stall and Ronald dropped in behind me from the other side. "Oh no..."

Then, it was Ronald's turn as he slid his fly down on his pants and speared me with his thick cock.

"OHHHHHHHHHH!!!" I grunted loudly as the mindless asshole fucked my asshole.

Outside the stall my cock was dripping the last remnants of my first cum shot of the evening and I heard the men's room door being unlocked.

"OH man, thanks, I need to pee real bad..." I heard the anxious sounding voice of a patron say as he hurried into the now unlocked men's room.

"AWWWWWWW..." I panted as Ronald thrust harder and harder and as deep as he possibly could into my poor sore anal canal.

"Say, what the hell is goin' on over there?" I heard the patron who had come into the men's room ask Alex.

"What's going on over there is tonight's main attraction here at the Local," I heard Alex reply.

"What's going on over here is outright violation!" I snarled loudly as Ronald now had my tits gripped in his fingertips and as he fucked me he pounded me hard against the stall door. "ARRRHHHHH, fucking twisted owners of this place stripped me out of my suit and tied me the fuck up in here...I'm being used here man!!!"

Outside the stall my cock did a stupid looking dance called the Twitch and Spasm as I was brutally fucked and manhandled.

"Shit Stud, sounds good to me," the bar patron said, his voice coming from a urinal where he was pissing heartily, relieving himself like a racehorse. "If that's what gets you your rocks off I got nothing against it..."

"NO, NO, wasn't my idea..." I blurted and then Ronald gripped my tits tighter and whispered in my ear that he was cumming, he was cumming, and he was fucking cumming.

His thick flood of warm creamy juices spurted from his cock and into my hole, mixing his mess with Alex's in there.

"HARRRRRRR..." he ranted and by now the way he was squeezing and twisting my tits was hurting like the devil.

"FUCKING rapist..." I ranted, my eyes squeezed tightly shut under my necktie turned blindfold.

When Ronald was done he finally let go of my tits and like Alex before him his cock slowly deflated and slid out of my hole. We were both breathless and I heard him quickly pack himself into his pants and zip up.

"My buddy is done in there Sir," I heard Alex saying to the bar patron who was now done pissing in the urinal. "Feel free to help yourself to my man Socks there any which was you choose to..."

"Yeah, Socks is right, looks like that's all he's got on is his Socks," the bar patron laughed and then Ronald climbed out of the stall and he and Alex left the men's room.

As I stood there trapped and feeling totally mortified I felt cum dripping out of my hole.

"Say Mister, if you're still out there and you can find it in your heart or some other part of you to untie me and get me out of this mess I sure as all fuck would appreciate it," I called out. "I got to say I'm feeling a bit sore and used up already in here and..."

But then, in reply the bar patron climbed up and over and into the stall with me...

"Fuck, fuck, look at you man, I knew that that meat stick of a cock out there had to be attached to a real muscle head..." the bar patron said, sounding breathless, one hand roaming over my back, my shoulders, my biceps, his other hand working at getting the zipper down on his pants.

When I heard the sound of his zipper slide down I braced myself...

"ARRRRRHHHHH!!!" I reeled as the bar patron, whoever the fuck he was entered me from behind with what felt like it had to be ten inches of prime thick beef. "OHHHHH you blasted fucker..."

"Not blasting yet Muscle head, but gimmie time, gimmie time here," the guy panted and with his hands now on my wide as a doorway shoulders he began getting into a good hard driving rhythm and he slid and thrust in and out of me. "Fucking great squishy hole you got here man..."

As he thrust harder each time he held tight to my shoulders, kissed the back of my neck and I felt his balls crashing against my lower ass cheeks. Obviously the bar patron had really freed himself from the confines of his pants. It got sleazier as he went on, he swore at me like a horned up marine (I wondered if he actually was a marine), starting not just kissing but also licking and bighting at the back of my neck and he gripped my shoulders tighter, really digging his fingertips into my flesh.

"OHHHHHHHHH...if I weren't blindfolded I would press charges against you Mister!" I croaked throatily.

"Press this Muscle head," the bar patron seethed and slammed every inch of his hard cock meat as deep as possible into my widening opening.

"AYYYYYRRRRRRR!!!" I cried out and tears formed in my eyes under my damned necktie turned blindfold. "Sadist!!!"

"Oh yeah, so I've been called Muscle hard, so I've been called..." the guy laughed and then I felt his juices flooding my hole.

Outside the stall my cock again twitched and danced, I felt it getting stiff again...betraying me again...

When the bar patron was done he thanked me for the use of my "great ass" as he called it and I heard him climb up and out of the stall.

"You're welcome fucker," I replied sarcastically, sweating miserably now.

I heard him leave the men's room but someone must have come in just as he was going out because just as I heard the door of the men's room close my cock was gobbled into a mouth outside the stall.

"OHHHHHHH..." I gasped at the suddenness of it, yet it was still feeling pretty good as I was sucked into a very saliva soaked mouth.

I felt the person drooling over my hard again manhood, their fingertips caressing my balls and then I was being sucked hard and sensually.

"MMMMMMM..." was all the person outside the stall said as he worked me with his mouth.

"Hey there, after you're done getting me off do you suppose you could untie me?" I asked with a grin. "I'm in a bit of a bind here, as you can see, and fuck, I can't see...guys blindfolded me in here too and..."

As he sucked me he shook his head "No" from side to side, jostling my cock back and forth as he did so...

"UHHHHHHHHH...okay fucker, have it your way," I panted. "I suppose I'm in no position to argue here...but please take it easy on my cock out there huh???"

Again he shook his head "No" from side to side, really hurting my poor manhood now. With his fingers he squeezed and tugged on my balls.

"HUUUUHHHHHHHHH..." I breathed deeply.

Well, at least this guy wasn't planning on fucking my poor asshole, he just seemed totally hell-bent on siphoning a load out of me... or so I thought...

"AAWWWWWHHHHH..." I groaned loudly and from the throat a short while later as I shot my load again, the guy holding my cock tight in one hand and my balls in the other as I spurted on the men's room floor. "OHHHHHHH FUCKING HELL of a feeling for a guy when he cums again so soon after cumming earlier..."

The guy chuckled and did his best to squeeze every drop of my juices from my cock...

Then, I realized I had been wrong, he did plan to fuck my asshole. Once I was done shooting my load the guy let of my manhood, climbed up the side and into the stall and buried his cock in me in what felt like no time.

"YUHHHHHHHHHH..." I gasped. "Not much for small talk are you bud?"

He grabbed the back of my head and shook it "No" from side to side.

"Didn't think so..." I said miserably. "OH MAN, my poor ass...looks like guys here tonight want my ass as well as my damned cock..."

When the guy shot his load inside me he bucked behind me, slapped my ass cheeks and when he was done he simply climbed out of the stall and was gone...as if he'd never been there to start with...

"FUCK, fuck, blasted owners of this goddamned joint..." I seethed, looking down in darkness and wiggling my toes as I sweated in my socks.

A short while later I heard the men's room door open yet again and a nerdy sounding male voice calling out, "Smith, Mister Smith? Mister Greg Smith?"

I looked up, rolled my eyes in my head under my blindfold and called out, "Yeah, unfortunately that would be me…Who the fuck wants to know?"

"Uh, well, you see, my name is Herbert Wilson and…" the guy called out.

"Uh well, actually I can't see Mister Herbert Wilson out there," I called back at him. "Besides tied to this stall door, as YOU CAN see, I'm fucking blindfolded in here as well."

"All the better, you see, I mean, you don't see, but I'm a salesman, having you tied and blindfolded works well for me, because of the product I'm here to demonstrate for you," the man named Herbert Wilson said.

I could not believe what I was hearing. This fucking guy actually wanted to sell me something?

"Uh, Mister, look, I'm really not in a position to be buying anything at the moment; my wallet is in my suit jacket out there and…" I began.

"Actually Mister Smith, you are in a position for what I need, you see, what I am selling is an erotic sexual device." Herbert Wilson said.

I gulped hard at the implications of what he had just said…and for some reason my cum sopped asshole twitched.

"I don't expect you to buy at the moment, but perhaps later when you're out of there and dressed and can get to your wallet you'll consider it…" the salesman said.

Again I rolled my eyes in disbelief under my blindfold.

"Mister, I tell you what, if you would be so kind as to untie me I'll consider looking at whatever the hell it is you're selling and…" I began again.

"Oh no, no, Mister Smith, the owners of the Local told me that before I tried to sell the device I had to give a firsthand demonstration to their bathroom model," Herbert said, sounding anxious as all hell.

Bathroom model???? BATHROOM MODEL??? Is that what Alex and Ronald were telling people that I was now??? Their goddamned bathroom model??? But before I could sound off about that to Mr. Wilson the salesman I heard him climbing up the side of the stall.

"Oh no..." I whispered miserably. "Pete, please get out from behind the bar and get me out of here..."

But that was not to be as I heard and felt Mr. Herbert Wilson land in the stall behind me and then he was feeling up my ass.

"Oh my, oh my indeed," he said, kneading and squeezing my globes as he admired them. "Mister Smith, you are the superb model for my newest device that I'm featuring in my store and on my website..."

"So glad to hear that..." I muttered angrily as the guy handled me as if I were not even human.

"First I'll fit the harness on you Mister Smith," Herbert Wilson said and I felt him pressed up behind me as he secured some sort of leather belt around my naked waist and then buckling it up behind me.

"Could you at least take the blindfold off me, even temporarily, so I can see what in the fucks it is you're making me wear here, Mister Wilson," I reeled through clenched teeth. "I honestly don't know what the owners told you about me but I assure you that I am not in this humiliating and blasted position by my own choice..."

"Well, they did say that besides being the bathroom model that you are a superb actor of sorts," the salesman stated. "And I must say you are playing your part rather well at this moment..."

I could not believe that anybody could be this naïve…or stupid for that matter…I mean, did the guy actually think that I wanted to be tied up to a stall door in a sleazy bar's men's room wearing just my damned socks and with my cock and balls on total display???

When Herbert was done the part of his device that he called the "harness" was strapped around my waist and I felt some sort of opening on it dangling just under my ass crack. More and more I did not like where this could be leading…

"Now for the main attraction Mister Smith," Herbert Wilson said. "I call this baby the Buzzer. It's going to make me a rich, rich man…"

"TH-the buzzer?" I asked, suddenly feeling very afraid, and very sucked on yet again as outside the stall another customer of the Local was in the men's room and sucking my cock. "UHHHHHHHHHHH…GAWD, hey Herbert, someone just slurped my pride and joy into their mouth out there…"

"Good, good Mister Smith, that will help a lot, seeing as when I insert the Buzzer it's best if you're being stimulated from the front end as well," he said merrily.

"Insert the Buzzer?" I asked. "OHHHHHHHH, easy with my cock out there huh whoever you are? I'm feeling a tad cooked in here already tonight…"

The person slowed down their pace and sucked me as if in slow motion…

"Herbert, I don't know what the fuck you're talking about, a buzzer or inserting it or…" I began and suddenly the stall area was filled with the sound of what could been a hive of bees that just flew upward, if you were a poor blindfolded guy that is. "HEY, what is that buzzing sound???"

"That Mister Smith is my moneymaker, and now I will insert it in your moneymaker," the obviously sleazy salesman said and then besides being sucked on I felt something else.

I felt as if the swarm of bees I mentioned was suddenly buzzing around in my shit chute.

"OH GOOD GAWWWWWD," I rasped loudly.

Herbert inserted the device one end into my very moist hole and the other end in the harness that was strapped around my waist. The harness would insure that the Buzzer would not slip from my hole.

"OHHHHHHHHHHH HOLY FUCKS," I rattled, goose bumps breaking out all over me.

"Herbert, what is that thing??? Get it out of my damned asshole!!!"

From outside the stall whoever was sucking my cock snickered meanly. I felt my cock tingling in the person's mouth. FUCK, but I was about to shoot a real splatter of a load let me tell you. That damned thing that Herbert Wilson called the Buzzer was cooking me bud. And it was also somehow spurring me on to shoot another good-sized load…and I would too…

I wiggled my ass real sexily, as much as I could in the bondage I was tied in and then whoever was outside the stall at my cock stopped sucking me…and began licking my balls.

"HUHHHHHHHHH…OH GAWD, whoever you are out there…don't stop now…" I pleaded. "With what this fucker in here just wedged up inside me I need to cum like gangbusters!"

But whoever he was he simply ignored me and went on licking and lapping at my sweaty balls. Fuck, I was being cum controlled now…first I was forced to shoot my load over and over…and now I was being put through denial…what a predicament I was in…

and that device buzzing in my shit chute was making me crazier and crazier with each passing moment.

"So Mister Greg Smith, what do you think?" Herbert Wilson asked me. "Is my device a sure thing where a moneymaker is concerned?"

"RRRRRRRRRRRR..." was all I could say as my teeth felt like they were vibrating in my head and my balls were licked and my cock twitched and ached to shoot that load.

"Yes, I agree totally Mister Smith," the salesman laughed. "The battery in the Buzzer is good for at least a couple of hours of continuous use. I'll allow you the pleasure of a free demonstration while you're in here."

"NO, NO, take it out, take this monstrosity out of my damned hole you sick excuse for a salesman..." I pleaded and he chuckled and gave my ass a friendly swat.

"I must say, the owners of this bar chose very well where you are concerned Mister Smith," Herbert Wilson said and then I heard him climbing out of the stall.

"OH FUCK, OH HOLY FUCKS..." I snarled and as whomever the hell it was that was licking balls went on and on at it I shot my load.

I shot my damned load without my cock being touched that time. I shot my load just from having my balls licked and my asshole buzzed...

"AYYYRRRRRRRRR..." I roared then, for when I was done creaming every part of me was more than alive, tingling and sensitized.

It's a known fact that after a guy shoots his load every part of him becomes overly sensitized and sensitive to the touch...especially his erogenous zones, and at that moment my main erogenous zone felt as if it was being fried...

"OHHHHHHHH my poor ass, someone get this thing out of me…" I cried, real tears soaking my blindfold by then.

The guy who had just licked my balls to the point of making me cum exited the men's room. I stood there feeling helpless and totally used and abused…

About an hour and a half later, by my best guess and estimates Alex was standing next to me in the cramped space of the stall. He had lowered my blindfold and it was dangling around my neck as I stood there still tied to the stall door while he fed me a much needed cool drink of water from a plastic bottle.

"There you go Socks, down the hatch," Alex said with a grin, one hand on the back of my head as I drank the water, the other hand holding the bottle to my trembling lips.

I was sopped in sweat, my calf length socks were stuck to my skin and I was feeling so very used up at that point. If Pete the bartender intended to take me home for romance after our dinner later that night I knew I would need the Viagra and vitamin supplements that Ronald had mentioned earlier upon him and Alex capturing me yet again…

My cock had been sucked to the point that it felt like it was the color purple as it still stuck out of the glory hole, tied tight. I had lost count of how many times I had been sucked. My balls weren't feeling so great either let me tell you. At some point I started shooting dry loads and that was when Alex was suddenly there. Probably someone told him that his "Bathroom Model" was starting to run dry…HAR, HAR, HAR… But no joke is when a poor guy starts shooting dry loads. As stated in the past, that, for some reason can really drive a guy over the edge.

Alex had been kind enough to take the "Buzzer" device out of my hole, the battery in it died sooner than Mister Herbert Wilson had predicted it would. The thing was out and the harness that had been strapped around my waist was gone too…good riddance I said…

"AHHHHH, th-thank you," I whispered when I was done slaking down the water that Alex was feeding me.

"No problem Socks ol' boy, can't have you dehydrating on us in here can we?" Alex quipped and gave my earlobe a suck. "Fucking hot dude you are Smith…"

"Alex, man, please, *please,* let me out of here *now*…it's been long enough tonight and…" I began to say, but suddenly my words were cut short as Alex grabbed a handful of my hair, yanked my head back and forced a tiny fifty milligram pill of Viagra into my open mouth. "ACCCHHHHHHHH!!!"

The pill rested on my tongue and then Alex pushed my head forward, pushed my chin up, closing my mouth and banged my forehead against the stall door.

"UUUUFFFFFF…" I gaped at the suddenness and atrocity of it the way he handled me.

"Swallow it Socks," Alex ordered, one hand on top of my head the other under my chin.

I gulped hard, the pill went down and my blindfold went back up over my eyes, courtesy of Alex…

"*Fucker…*" I whispered miserably and waited for the Viagra tablet to start setting in.

Snickering meanly Alex slid his newly hard cock between my cheeks and began fucking me for his second time that night.

"OHHHHHHHHHHRRRR SHIT and the Viagra didn't even kick in yet," I grunted sarcastically.

"No problem on that either Socks," Alex laughed as he thrust his rod deep inside me, so deep that it felt as if it would slide through me and come out of my mouth. "I locked the men's room door from the inside. No one will suck your cock till that little pill takes effect…look at this as I'm just helping you to kill time…HA!!!"

With that he spewed a hearty mess of cum inside me; slapping my ass cheeks as he came and came…swearing like a marine, filling me to the brim of my poor overused a-hole…

"FUCKING BASTARD…" I swore as the guy climbed out of the stall yet again, leaving me there dripping cum from my asshole all over again…EMBARRASSING as all hell.

Once Alex unlocked the door to the men's room and walked out the sleazy action started all over again bud. The Viagra kicked in, my cock stiffened, was sucked and that was the end of the dry loads…for the moment. Once more cock hungry guys were scoffing down my homemade protein drinks…GAWD…

When I had been in that stall for nearly three and a half hours I heard a familiar voice in the men's room.

"Man, I've been behind that bar since Alex and Ronald opened this dump tonight," the voice said and I smiled from ear to ear behind my blindfold. "This is the first break I've had all night. If I didn't get in here I swear I would have pissed behind the bar…"

It was Pete, the bartender, the guy that was hopefully still taking me to dinner that night. God knew at that point I was hungrier than I had ever felt in my life before. After the way I had been sexed over this time in that stall I could eat a steer bud, just as someone planned on eating me at that moment. While Pete went on talking to whoever he was pissing beside at the urinals I heard someone climb into the stall and land behind me. They squeezed my ass cheeks and in a disguised voice whispered, "Ah, dinner is served."

I didn't need three guesses to know what that meant. My asshole was about to be savagely eaten. Well, I had had enough and rescue was just outside the stall. Once Pete knew that the poor guy all tied up in the stall was yours truly I had no doubt he would free me.

"Pe..." I was about to call out but the person in the stall chose that goddamned moment to shove what I guessed was an old used sock in my mouth. "RRRMMMFFFF..."

The person forced the stinking sock deep into my craw and then tied its mate over it, jamming it tightly in place.

"Hmm, looks like Alex and Ronald got someone in the stall tonight," I heard Pete say and my heart sank as my ass started being eaten by whoever was in the stall.

"Hope you're having fun in there!" Pete called out.

"Want to take a few sucks?" I heard Pete's buddy ask him.

"Nah, being that I work here I can't fraternize with the other help," Pete said. "Besides, I got a dinner date later tonight with that hot suit guy that was here earlier. He's fucking beautiful and I plan to suck him...I plan to suck him till he's bone dry..."

As whoever it was ate my ass my heart hammered in my chest and my cock twitched long and hard outside the stall door...

Fuck me hard bud, but if Pete planned on sucking me as he had just said I figured he would need that bottle of Viagra and vitamin supplements that Ronald had taunted me with earlier...JEEZ...

As the person in the stall with me at that moment went on eating and slurping at my mangy asshole I pulled myself to my socked toes and wiggled uncontrollably...

The Local closes, like most other bars in the city, at four AM...

It was three thirty AM when I felt the ropes around my cock and balls being undone and then the ropes binding me to the stall door were untied. As the ropes fell away from my body the first thing I did was reached up to take my necktie turned blindfold away from my eyes and then I angrily untied the sock that was holding the other sock in my mouth as a makeshift gag. Whoever was doing the good deed of untying me undid the knots in the ropes around my feet and then I was free... I glanced down at the rancid socks I was holding in my hand and saw that they were a pair of OTC (over the calf) length nylon navy blue numbers. Obviously I had been gagged by either some sort of corporate executive or perhaps even an off-duty cop...JEEZ...

I took a few steps back, breathing hard and slowly slid my cock and balls out of the glory hole and into the stall. When I saw my most private of parts I smiled gratefully. With a trembling hand I unlatched the stall door and shambled out of the small prison. My cock was deflated and shriveled. I had been sucked just about dry. My balls were aching from having been so brutally drained and my asshole felt as wet as a sponge from all the fucking fucks I had endured back there. I saw my suit laid out on a sink, my shoes on the floor under the sink and lo and fucking behold, even my under shorts were there. It looked like Alex had decided not to keep them as a souvenir this time... As I pulled them on I thought how I would not have to free-ball in my suit for my date with Pete the bartender.

It took me a good twenty minutes or so to dress myself, seeing as I was feeling sexually exhausted and my hands would not stop trembling. It took me five minutes just to smooth out my tie and redo it around the collar of my shirt. Once I was fully dressed I pissed long and hard into a urinal, washed my hands, splashed some cold water on my face and exited the men's room...

As I walked down the short hallway from the men's room back to the bar I saw Alex and Ronald seated at their usual spot where they usually were just before closing. I saw the last two customers heading for the exit of the bar. The two customers glanced at me, snickered and made their exit. I clenched my teeth in anger, figuring that they had been two of the sleazy perverts who'd had at me this night while I had been tied up in the stall.

When I looked behind the bar I saw Pete rinsing out some glasses. He didn't see me as I made my way over, for which I was glad in a way. I didn't want him knowing that it had been me in that stall that night… Alex and Ronald mockingly thanked me and went to their private office to tally up the night's receipts, asking Pete to lock up the bar when he left…

When Pete left with me he was carrying me over his shoulder, seeing as I looked totally exhausted…

"We'll go to my place Greg," Pete said with a smile as he lugged me toward his car. "I don't know why but for some reason you look totally beat to shit…"

I told him I was appreciating the ride to his car as he lugged me along and was glad I didn't have to be at work the next day…I planned to stay with Pete for the duration…

YOU'RE FIRED!

Written by Justin Tyler-Ormond

This story actually begins about two years ago when Anthony Alberti was the manager of a men's furnishing store of fine suits and formal wear for men. At the time, Tony had working for him a young punk named Frank, who went by the street name of Slash. This kid was always screwing things up, but Tony thought that with the proper mentoring and training he could reform the kid. Regardless of his efforts though, Tony eventually needed to fire Slash. Besides screwing things up, Slash would scare customers out of the store- it was as though he had Tourettes Syndrome, a condition that made him yell and scream obscenities at the customers. Slash vowed revenge on Tony, because he was unable to find another job, and he felt that his life basically went down the toilet because of being fired. And because of being fired at the hands of that fucking well-dressed bastard no less, Tony wound up homeless. He hung around on the streets with other misfits, and for the most-part was always either drunk or stoned out of his mind.

Tony of course did not give the threat a second thought, because as a store manager he was responsible for the hiring and firing of personnel. Besides, what was this street punk really going to do to him? Slash was often all talk and no action. Slash, unable to forgive or forget, felt that the next time that his and Tony's paths crossed, it would be different.

He would make sure the job was done to the end…

Present Day…

Tony was a hunk of a guy. At thirty-one years old, with smooth bronze skin and long blond hair that he wore in a tightly pulled back ponytail. Tony was the envy and desire of many men and women. His eyes would melt the soul of anyone he looked at. They were a deep hue of green, with long eyelashes that offset his hypnotic stare. He worked out every other day and he always ate health-conscious foods. Needless to say, he was in great shape. He had broad shoulders, six-pack abs, a narrow waist, a rock hard ass that you could bounce a coin off, yes, he was the complete package, and had a very nice "package" that swung between his ample, well-muscled thighs. Tony knew this and would often flaunt his assets. This usually meant that he wore clothes that were formfitting or very snug, so that everyone could see his wonderful body definition, the muscles rippling under each garment. Tonight, however, was a bit different. He would be suiting up, from head to toe, to the nines as the saying went.

Tony was going to the opening night of the opera. He was impeccably dressed in a new Versace tuxedo with all the trimmings. He had spent a fortune on the tuxedo, and another fortune having it altered to fit him the way he wanted it to fit. This was New York City after all, and the opening of the opera. The tuxedo was a traditional one, in black. What made it special was the actual cut of the garment. It was a European cut, which meant the jacket was broad and padded at the shoulders, tapered at the waist and the pants were finely detailed with a triple pleated front. The pants were fitted to show off Tony's abundant manhood. Ample thigh room very tapered in the legs and a bit longer in length so that the slacks laid perfectly in the front, just enough to show off his soft black Italian leather shoes. His shirt was made of white French handkerchief linen, very soft, and form fitting to his body. You could even make out the outline of Tony's nipples through the shirt; this was due to the formfitting fabric and the sheer nature of the shirt linen. He put on his finest gold and black onyx shirt studs and cufflinks. They had diamonds set in the middle of each piece. Tony had everything ready with the exception of his overcoat. Earlier in the week he had purchased a cream-colored lynx coat from a furrier located in the mall near his home. The coat, which he requested be altered, was late in being completed, which meant that Tony had to pick it up on his way to the opera. This was going to make the time schedule very tight for him. The opera started at eight PM, and the coat was not going to be ready until six PM that evening. Being Sunday, the mall was going to close earlier than it usually did during the week.

Suited up, with his opera tickets safely tucked away in an inside pocket of his beautifully tailored tuxedo Tony raced to the shopping center and pulled into the parking lot near the furrier's store. He whipped his new convertible sports car, a white Lexus, into the first open space he saw in the lot. In doing so, he cut off a bunch of punks. They were in a beat up Jeep Wrangler and were trying to park in the very same space that Tony had just slid into. The punks uttered obscenities at Tony, who in return flipped them the finger. He was in a rush; he had more important things on his mind and could not be bothered with these assholes.

Strutting into the mall, Tony went directly to the furrier and picked up his coat. The shop was closing for the night, and so, he was unable to try the garment on in the store. Practically meeting him at the door and rushing him out the second the coat was in his hands, the saleswoman immediately locked up after escorting Tony out. He had given the furrier such a hard time about the coat; they just wanted to be done with him. So Tony took the coat and headed for the nearest men's room so that he could see how the thick expensive fur looked with his tuxedo. Pleased with what he saw, it was detailed just as he had demanded. Double-breasted, high-collared, with a broad lapel, thick cuffs and full-length, with a long sash belt to tie the coat at the waist- it was perfect! Tony posed, looking in the full-length mirror of the men's room and admired how he looked wearing the coat. The coat gave off a cream shine, and was as plush as could be. The weight of it on his shoulders felt wonderful. It was warm and supple. It was everything he wanted it to be. It framed his black tuxedo just as he had imagined it would. He adjusted his thick golden ponytail over the high collar. He could not wait to get back to his car, where a pair of skin-tight, lamb soft leather gloves was waiting for him along with a long white silk scarf. The thought of all this gave Tony an erection. The outfit would be complete, and with that he knew he would turn every head at the performance tonight. Glancing at his Rolex he decided that that he only had a few more minutes to spare before he had to race off to make his engagement. Unbeknownst to Tony, the hoodlums had followed him into the mall, and were now stalking him. They watched the dapper guy's every move. They had watched him from the parking lot, into the mall and then to the men's room.

As he was looking at himself in the mirror one of the punks came into the men's room. Tony paid him no attention; because he was too busy admiring himself. One by one the other gang members came into the men's room until there were five of them in there, including Slash. He was obviously the leader of this punk gang. They left one of their friends outside the men's room to keep everyone else out. Without Tony knowing it happened the punks formed a ring around him. When he finally did realize it he questioned them as to what the meaning of this was. They snickered and told him they did not like the fact that he took their parking space and then flipped them off. Tony, in his arrogant way told them to get a life, and to get over it. The lead punk, Slash, said this was big talk coming from a long-haired sissy boy who dressed like a homo.

By now the punks were advancing on him. Even up close Tony did not recognize Slash. However Slash immediately recognized his old boss, or Bossman, as he would refer to Tony when he had been working for him. At this point Tony was becoming angrier by the second and had just about had all he could take from these street urchins. He had to get to the opera; he didn't have the time for their shit. Parking space indeed, and being flipped off, these guys should be used to that Tony thought. But the gang members continued to taunt him about the way he was dressed, and how his cologne made him smell like a girl. In reality, Tony's cologne was the very manly scent of Drakkar Noir, but he may have been a bit liberal with it tonight. Regardless, the scent would not hold for much longer, not with what these punks had planned for this muscle-headed, snot-nosed pretty boy. The punks taunted and teased Tony, flinging names at him one after another.

As the harassment continued Tony decided that these kids were no match for his well-muscled form, so he reached back to take a swipe at one of them. But there was no way that Tony was going to make the punch connect, for as he reached back, one of the punks grabbed his arm and deftly twisted it behind his back. Then, as Tony could not believe what had just happened another punk quickly grabbed his other arm and twisted that one behind his back also. Tony tried to squirm out of their hold, but he did not want to fight too much, because he was afraid he might rip his expensive overcoat, tuxedo jacket, or shirt. The two punks holding Tony's arms spun him around to the middle of the room and hurled him to the floor. Before he could even react Tony wound up face-first on the floor. The floor was wet and slimy, rather dirty for a public mall toilet, but, after all, it was the end of a very high traffic day.

Tony quickly tried to get up but a large heavy work boot came down on his back, while another booted foot kicked him in the side. As Tony lay on the floor he heard the familiar sound of someone pissing, but the piss was hitting something that was not a toilet or urinal. He suddenly realized that one of the punks was pissing on his new lynx fur coat. The guy was laughing and spraying his hot piss all over the backside of the thick coat. The punk kept at it for some time, letting his golden liquid soak in real well. The guy must have stored his piss all day Tony thought. Cursing now and spitting in anger Tony again tried to get up, but he was kicked down, this time in the other side. He made a sound of "OOOFFF" and then someone else was now pissing on his coat. Actually, by now, all the urchins had whipped out their dirty cocks and were pissing on Tony, spraying him down. They were pissing not only on his coat, but also on his once perfectly coiffed hair, causing streams of hot piss to run down his handsome face and onto the tight arrow collar of his crisp white tuxedo shirt.

As the pissing subsided Tony tried again to get to his feet, only to find that the floor was so wet and slimy that he could not get his balance. He felt his feet slipping from under him as he made an attempt to stand. He fell to the floor in a sitting position. However, as he fell, he heard the sound of something ripping. The crotch seam of his pants gave way a bit when he had hit the tiled floor. As Tony sat on the floor, in a bit of shock, Slash grabbed him by his ponytail and started to drag the poor guy across the bathroom. Tony screamed in pain and could feel the wet slime soaking through his pants now. He tried to beat on Slash's hands to get him to stop dragging him. All this accomplished though was to rip the seams of Tony's form-fitting shirt where the sleeves and the shoulders met. He could not get enough force to have any effect on the gang leader. Slash began to pull Tony closer now, still holding him by his ponytail, toward one of the urinals on the wall. Forcibly shoving Tony's head into the urinal Slash proceeded to flush it a number of times, causing the water to flow over Tony's face and soak into his thick hair. Spitting and moaning, Tony struggled to free himself, but in the long run only caused the seams of his imported tuxedo to split even more. Hearing the sound of the arms almost separating under Tony's evening coat Slash let go. Happy with what he had done to him so far, Slash stood over his prey, smiling from ear to ear. Finally able to stand, Tony was now wincing too much from the pain of having his hair almost pulled out by its roots and in too much shock as well to do any fighting. His sides ached where he had been kicked. The urinal water coated Tony's smooth tan skin, mixing with the urine that had been pissed and sprayed on him only minutes before. The fluids matted down his thick hair, causing his ponytail to stick to the back of his neck and lay limp along the collar of his fur coat, which, sadly, was also soaked. The sound of piss dripping down the back of his coat, from where all five punks had pissed on him rang in Tony's ears. In more ways than one- he was pissed.

In the background Tony heard one of the punks saying something about him being an animal killer. Before long, all the punks were taunting him about wearing fur, and the cruelty of it. One of the snot-nosed kids pulled out a knife and said he was going to get a trophy tonight. With great skill the punk dug the tip of the knife into the arm of Tony's fur coat and sliced the sleeve from the shoulder to the thick cuff. He then pulled and yanked until the sleeve came free from the body of the coat. As the sleeve came off so did the sleeve's lining, exposing Tony's tuxedo jacket arm. One of the other punks did the same thing to the other arm of Tony's coat, yanking and tugging until it came free. Both sleeves were now gone on Tony's nine thousand five hundred dollar coat. Enraged beyond anything he had ever felt before, Tony lunged at one of the punks that was holding one of the severed sleeves, but he was tripped by yet another gang member. With a shove to his back, again, Tony quickly found himself laying face-first on the slimy wet floor. He felt many hands on his back now, clawing and cutting at his fur coat. The vent in the back of the garment gave way from all the tugging, splitting the coat up the back, from the hem to the thick high collar. The sound of the pelts being ripped apart just about made Tony cry. He could see the ripped chunks of fur and the smooth silk lining being thrown all over the place.

The ripping only stopped when there was no more coat left on Tony's back. The thick collar with its wide lapel was shredded off in one good pull, the stitches popping one by one. The deep silk-lined pockets were ripped away, causing the contents to spill out onto the tiled floor. Slash took the sash belt and put it around his own waist and stated that this was one of his trophies. The other punks scooped up the loose items that were once inside the now torn pockets. Sprinkled all over the floor were a set of car keys to a brand new Lexus, a metal tin of designer breath mints, a silver hair comb, a cell phone and a gold cigar case- it was a veritable treasure trove of top-of-the-line accessories.

The punks started kicking Tony again. All he could do to protect himself was to curl up into a ball. One of the punks grabbed Tony's legs, while another grabbed his arms. They stretched him out on the floor so that he was now lying on his back, and with some rope they had they tied Tony's arms to the pipes under the sink. His legs they tied to the toilet stalls. Tony was absolutely helpless now, and not to mention a tad terrified. The urchins were swarming around him, rubbing their hands over his chest and crotch. Even in the frightened state Tony was in he could not help getting a hard-on as his cock and balls were being rubbed through his silk tuxedo pants. As the punks were rubbing Tony's crotch one of them started pissing on him again. This time Tony was pissed on all over his white tuxedo shirt and smooth tan face.

Tony's French linen shirt went transparent from the wetness. His pierced nipple was fully exposed, even though his shirt was covering it. One of the punks noticed this and said, "Hey guys, look here!" and with his knife, sliced Tony's shirt open at the nipple. The punk then ripped the shirt open from the slice and started to fondle Tony's gold nipple ring. Another of the punks said, "Let's see what's on the other side." He reached under the tuxedo jacket and grabbed the shirt from the tear at the armhole. The punk yanked hard and tore the front half of Tony's shirt right off, exposing his smooth bronzed pecs. Another nipple ring was to be found. The punk that was fondling Tony's nipple piercing said, "He looks better that way," and proceeded to rip the rest of the front of the dapper guy's shirt off. All that was now left to the shirtfront was the placard that held the shirt studs in place. Tony's black silk cummerbund remained tight around his partially exposed abs.

Once this had happened all the punks started to go to work on Tony's tuxedo. With their knives they made slices in his pants and put their fingers in the holes…and RIIIIPPPPPP, the pants were torn down to the cuff and up to the waist. Not one hole was made, but many and they were ripped open violently. The fronts of Tony's tuxedo pants were shredded to thin slices. His bright red silk boxer shorts were now exposed for all to see. They were wet from the floor slime, and from Tony having been pissed on. While his pants were being shredded Tony's tuxedo jacket was receiving similar punishment. One of the punks tore the satin lapels on the jacket so they were left to just dangle in the air. The polished black buttons on the front of the jacket were each popped off, one at a time, clattering to the tiled floor. The breast pocket was ripped out causing the white silk pocket square to fall to the wet floor. The two lower pockets were yanked on until the stitching gave way and the smooth silk lining was exposed in each. The jacket lining was then ripped out, and the sleeves were shredded into many pieces before eventually being torn off the jacket. Slash forcibly pulled the remains of Tony's jacket off his body, quickly followed by the pleated cummerbund being torn off and tossed across the tiled floor. He then grabbed what remained of Tony's shirt, and stripped it off the man in one quick yank. The force was so great that the cuff-linked French cuffs remained around Tony's wrists and the arrow collar with the black silk bowtie stayed in place around his muscled neck. The rest of the shirt was gone. Tony's hand-tied bowtie was drooping around his neck. Slash put an end to the tie and collar by slicing them off in one quick cut. Next, Slash put his hand under Tony's hard muscled ass and started massaging it. Searching and finding the tear that had been made in Tony's pants when he fell Slash took hold of the torn material, and with one long hard, audible RIIIPPPPPP, ripped the back of

Tony's pants off. Tony now only had half a pair of pants on. One muscled leg was completely exposed, while the shredded fabric covered his other leg. Slash stepped to the other side, and again feeling under Tony's ass, ripped the other half of the man's pants off, completely exposing his silk boxers.

At this point one of the punks started to riffle through the torn remains of Tony's tuxedo that was scattered all about. He pocketed a wad of cash that he took out of Tony's leather wallet and then tossed the wallet to the floor. Next he ripped the gold and diamond studs off the shredded shirtfront that was lying at his feet. He noticed the matching cufflinks were still on Tony's wrists, and with the knife he sliced the cuffs off and pocketed the links. Then, he undid the gold Rolex and slapped it onto his own wrist, smiling as he thought about all the drugs and booze he could buy once he pawned all this stuff. In one last act of cruelty the punk reached down and popped the golden rings out of Tony's piercing's, giving each of the man's nipples a rather rough tug and twist, causing Tony to buck and moan in a man's pain.

A second punk reached down and gathered up the tossed wallet and checked it over once more. Turning to the first thief he laughed aloud and said, "It looks like this snot-nosed pretty boy was going to see some freaking fairies sing tonight!" With that the punk took the single ticket Tony had spent months trying to obtain for the opera opening and tossed it into the nearest urinal, flushing it several times. The punk just stood there laughing as he watched the paper ticket dissolve in the urinal water.

Yet the punks felt that this was still not enough humiliation for Tony. Slash couldn't have agreed more. Two of the punks took hold of Tony's red silk boxers by the fly and pulled as hard as they could. RIIIIIPPPPP! The boxers were wrenched from Tony's body. One boxer ripper, while still holding the torn silk, dropped his jeans and began stroking his own dick that he now had wrapped in the expensive fabric. He was hard in a moment's time. He jacked himself off and shot his load all over Tony's face and hair, the hot load of jizz erupting from the punk's cock in a thick fountain. The other boxer ripper did the same thing. This time though the first punk held Tony's mouth open so, as the second punk jacked off and shot his load, his thick load of cum ended up squirting into Tony's gaping mouth and sliding down his dry tongue. It coated his now hoarse throat.

Slash then told the punks to flip Tony over. They untied one of his arms and legs and the retied them so that now he was lying on his stomach. Slash informed Tony that he had this coming. With that he proceeded to drop his pants, whipping his hardened cock out. Mounting Tony, Slash started fucking the man raw, sliding his thick uncut cock into Tony's smooth muscled ass in one quick stroke. Slash grunted and moaned as he felt Tony's hole clamping down around his thick cock. Tony started to yell, but one of the punks picked up a piece of the torn fur topcoat and stuffed it into Tony's mouth in order to gag him. Slash began to thrust his stiff rod into Tony's ass, riding him hard and fast. Tugging on Tony's ponytail, he proceeded to buck and moan with each powerful thrust of his throbbing cock. Slash's hot cum filled Tony's ass, and was overflowing out of the dapper guy's asshole in seconds. Slash told the punks to flip Tony over again. They did so. Then, one at a time, they took turns stroking Tony's hardened cock and massaging his clean shaven balls. Even though Tony was in pain from having been fucked so roughly and worked over, he could not help but get a massive erection. His mind was racing from having five guys working his bound body over, stroking his cock, tugging on his balls. Within a few minutes Tony shot his load. He came spurting out of his thick cut cock, smearing and dripping all over his abs, chest, and down the veined shaft of his manhood. The lucky guy who was stroking Tony's cock at the time he blew his thick load wiped his seed-slicked hands off on Tony's discarded silk cummerbund. After all, the punk thought to himself, it was called a cum merbund for a good reason.

Finally, looking down at Tony's cum-covered, piss-soaked bound body Slash told the punks that their job was done. With that announcement made they took the remains of Tony's ripped clothing and stuffed it down the toilets. One of the punks liked the looks of Tony's Italian leather shoes and pulled them off him. Another punk took out his knife and sliced Tony's sheer black OTC socks in half. The urchin then took the torn socks and tied the handles of the toilets with them, causing them to constantly run. The clothes were not going to go down the toilets, and with the handles being tied down with Tony's long socks it caused the toilets to clog and overflow. Tony was left tied to the floor of the men's room with water rushing over his completely naked body. The punk who had taken Tony's shoes pounded the base of his expensive dress pump into the full-length mirror of the men's room, causing it to shatter into jagged shards all over the floor. The punks then ran from the men's room, laughing and shouting, leaving poor Tony to fend for himself. The dapper guy who no longer felt so dapper struggled to break free from his bindings, but was more than afraid to move too quickly for fear the mirror shards would cut his naked form to ribbons. The punk who had been left to guard the door finally got a chance to look in the men's room to see what had been done. Disappointed he had missed all the fun he took a knife from his pocket and chopped off Tony's thick ponytail- which had taken Tony several years to grow to its generous length. The punk figured it would be an awesome reminder, for both the gang and this "pretty boy", of what had occurred here tonight.

With the punks long gone, the water flowed and began to seep out of the men's room, flooding the mall concourse. Being near closing time a janitor was walking by on his final rounds of the day, and seeing the water gushing out from under the doorway he entered the men's room. He was shocked at what he saw. He was so shocked that all he could do was run out of the men's room as quickly as he had entered and get mall security. He did not even try to shut the water off. Tony yelled to the janitor but it was too late, the door had already closed and the guy was on his way for help. Tony, still nervous about the glass shards that were now jabbing his naked form was surprisingly relieved when the janitor left, because he was mortified, totally embarrassed about being found tied up, naked and with cum still dripping from his semi-erect cock. He struggled, again, to try to free himself, but failed, giving in to the thought that he would indeed need someone else to help him get out of this infernal mess.

Within minutes a crowd had formed around the men's room, but no one was willing to go in because of the water and glass shards seeping from the door left ajar. Sounds of a man moaning were also spilling out of the bathroom. Finally, the janitor returned with mall security. One of the security guards attempted to break up the forming crowd, but they all still lingered around, wondering what the problem was. The second guard and the janitor went into the men's room. The janitor stopped the water from running while the security guard started to cut Tony free from his bonds.

Tony attempted to explain to the security guard what had happened. However, the guard was hesitant to believe him, the story sounding too surreal to be considered factual since there was no real evidence of the punks having ever been there. At first the guard officially agreed with Tony, but he really felt it was some sort of prank or even a drug deal that went bad...very bad. The guard started to even convince himself that what Tony spoke of only happened in the movies or during some erotic fantasy chat in cyber land. He should know, having surfed those chat rooms often enough himself the guard thought. But, could this guy be for real? Could he??? How could the guard explain away the fact that this guy was tied down by all fours? The janitor was also quick to point out to the guard the shreds of expensive material he was now withdrawing from the clogged toilets.

Since Tony had no clothes to put on, the janitor ran and got him an old dirty pair of coveralls and then sent the once dapper guy on his way, telling him that major repairs would have to be done for all the damage that was caused here. Gang or no gang, the place was trashed and as far as the janitor was concerned Tony had played a very big role in all of it. Deciding that this was turning into quite a spectacle the security guards started to clear the area of the mall employees and last-minute shoppers that were hanging around-Tony included. A story like this would be bad press for the mall. This needed to be cleaned up quickly, before the rumors spread. There was no way for Tony to dry himself off, or to even clean himself up at this point. He just put the coveralls on over his wet and cum encrusted body and exited the bathroom.

As he walked out of the men's room the dwindling crowd started to whisper and point, with others even going as far as to stop and laugh at him. They did not know what had happened; all they saw was a disheveled wet man in coveralls, walking barefoot out of the bathroom, with one of the security guards motioning behind him, the hand gesture implying that Tony was just a little crazy. The crowd took the hint and cleared out, glancing over their shoulders to get a good look at the guy, which they would later refer to as, the mumbling freak with the wild look in his eyes and the really fucked up hair. Tony couldn't remember a more embarrassing moment in his life. He was mortified for the second time this evening. Words failed to describe how truly horrible he felt.

Tony tried to get to the nearest exit as fast as possible, but since it was now well past closing time for a good portion of the mall; most of the exits were locked. He had to walk to the farthest point in the mall, barefooted, and then go through a major department store to get out. What made matters worse was that he had to ask employees where the exit was. Men and women that he had just dealt with only days ago as he purchased items for this very evening looked at him like he was a lunatic of some sort. There was no way for Tony to leave unnoticed. The whispering and pointing continued as he made his way to the exit.

Walking through the cold damp parking lot, Tony thought about what had just occurred. Shaking his damp head he couldn't figure out why this had happened to him. In a daze, practically stumbling over to his car he suddenly realized he had no wallet or keys. But, to make matters worse, adding insult to injury as the saying goes; he found that the convertible top of his car had been slashed to shreds. Also, the body of the car looked like someone had taken a baseball bat to it. The hood and trunk were dented in, and the four tires were flat. All of the windows were smashed and it looked like the gas tank was leaking. The driver side door was ajar and it appeared that someone had taken one of the parking lot garbage cans and dumped the contents of it into the car. Empty food wrappers and half-full bottles littered the once pristine, all white leather interior of the trashed car.

Tony did not know what to do next. Everything was ruined. He stood there thinking that maybe this would be enough evidence for the security guards to help him. Then, suddenly, as he stood there lost in thought, Slash snuck up behind the once dapper guy, and with all his brute strength grabbed the back of the coveralls. RIIIIIIPPPPPP was the sound, the tearing of the garment off Tony's body. Slash left him standing there in shock, naked again. As he ran by Tony with the torn coveralls in his hand, Slash yelled, "You mother fucker, are fired! Lets see how you deal with it bitch!" Then, Slash put his cigarette lighter to the coveralls and threw them into Tony's trashed car. The car immediately became engulfed in flames. As Slash hopped into the gang-filled jeep that was parked nearby he continued to yell, waving Tony's wallet in the air.

"And by the way asshole, we know where you live, you fucker!" Slash ranted. "Your house is toast too, Boss man!"

With that Tony collapsed onto the cold ground, naked and mentally drained. Moaning to himself he finally realized who Slash was, but was helpless to do anything about it, because he could not remember the punk's real name. Still in shock, Tony began to realize that he had been beaten down. Just like Slash, he was now a street punk with nothing, nothing at all, but the pain and humiliation of the evening…

PHOTO SHOOT

Written by Ron Bossman

I had seen this guy's ad on AOL and I was looking for someone to take some new pictures of me for my profile. We chatted on and off several times. We found out that we were both very interested in role-play scenes. As luck would have it we were both into bondage, toys, etc. We decided to do a role-play/photo shoot.

We set the scene up in advance. I would be an agency model who was coming over to fill in for someone who had called in sick. I had no idea what the shoot was about. I was told that I had better do a good job. I was told to make the photographer happy.

I got to his studio right on time. It was a great space. We started the shoot in my street clothes. He took several shots of me in different positions. Then he told me to take my shirt off. So far so good, this would be easy. He took more pictures, very sexy pictures of me showing off my muscular chest, my washboard abs and my big fleshy and pointy nipples. He told me exactly how to pose, where he wanted me to stand, to sit, etc.

Next he wanted me to take my sweatpants off. I was now just in my underwear. I was kind of uncomfortable but there wasn't anyone else there, just me and him. He took tons of pictures of me in my underwear, white boy briefs to be exact.

He then told me he wanted me to try on a few other outfits for him. He showed me to a side bedroom where a pile of clothes was laid out on the bed. It looked like tee shirts and underwear. He told me to try some on and then to come out when I was ready. So, I went through the stuff and put on a tee shirt. It was torn in several places. The same with a pair of briefs I found. I tried to pick a pair that covered most of my private parts then came out for him to photograph me. He loved the shots. He took a break and started ripping the underwear in several places. Jeez, I was practically hanging out of them now. I tried my best not to say anything, remembering that I had been told to make him happy.

He sent me back to the side bedroom several times to change outfits. There wasn't much left except for the real skimpy stuff. I was forced to come out this time in a G-string. It barely covered anything whatsoever; I may as well have been totally nude. It was really very embarrassing for me but he loved it and he took pictures of me in several positions.

Then, the photographer decided that he wanted to take pictures of me lifting weights. I followed him down a hall, still wearing just the G-string. He led me into a room that was set up like a gym. He told me to start working out, so I did. It felt weird working out in a G-string in front of him. I got on the weight bench and began doing chest presses and before I knew it he was kneeling in front of me, getting a great shot of my basket. Then lo and fucking behold he took out two pairs of wrist restraints. As I set the weight bar down I asked him what the devices were for, as if I didn't know. He smiled and said they were just props. I was hesitant man but he was insistent. So, I wound up with each of my wrists strapped tight to each arm of the bench. My chest was nice and pumped up from the workout I had just done and he took tons of pictures. Then, he peeled my G-string off. I wanted to prevent him from doing that, but being restrained the way I was made it impossible of course. I told him that I didn't want pictures of me naked but he ignored me. I started struggling at that point but of course I could not get free from the wrist restraints. Then, to my dismay he took picture after picture after picture of me buck naked and struggling. He loved it.

Next he grabbed one of my ankles and pulled it up and over my head. HOLY FUCK! He locked my ankle in place next to my wrist. He then did the same to my other ankle. GOD! My ass was now sticking straight up and it was wide open. I kept asking him what the fuck he was doing, telling him to stop. Again he loved it and he just kept on taking pictures. (To be truthful here we had set up a code word for him to really stop if I wanted him to. If I used the word all play would stop for sure.) So meanwhile he was taking tons and tons of pictures.

He left the room and came back with several dildos and butt-plugs. I was protesting big time now, but it was no use. He slowly greased up my asshole, working his slicked fingers in there, driving me batty, getting me nice and lubed up. In between he stopped several times to take pictures of my now moist ass crevice. Then, when I was good and sopped up back there he worked a dildo into me. It was one with a long handle at the end of it. The camera was able to get a good shot of the handle sticking out of my ass, JEEZ.

Man, this was embarrassing. He then replaced the dildo with a butt-plug and let me up. Man, I was moaning and groaning in a man's agony/ecstasy let me tell you. He led me over to the middle of the room, raised my hands above my head and attached the wrist restraints to chains that were hanging from the ceiling. Now my arms were raised and wide apart.

He then put shackles around each of my ankles. He attached them to hooks in the floor. Again my legs were spread wide; the damned plug was still in my ass, tormenting me. He then got a parachute ball-stretcher device and as I ranted and protested in his face he attached the damned thing to my balls, GAWD! Then, with a chain he hooked the parachute ball-stretcher to another hook that was in the floor. My poor balls were pulled tight. He added a slave collar around my neck and then blindfolded me. FUCK, I was in complete bondage hell now…and he was taking tons of pictures.

As I stood there in darkness I heard the sound of a doorbell ring. (We had talked about adding a third party but didn't have any firm plans, so this was a surprise.) Whoever they were they came up the stairs. Then all was quiet.

All of a sudden I felt hands on my chest. Fingers grabbed and pinched my man-sized nipples. As I was moaning and being felt up I heard the clicking of the camera. The photographer was taking pictures of me being used now as a sex toy. My balls were being tugged on. I felt the butt-plug being pulled from my ass, only to be replaced by a condom-covered hard dick. Whoever he was he pumped me for the camera, fucking me real good.

Then, I was taken down but still blindfolded. The photographer (or so I supposed it was him) locked my hands behind my back, leaving the slave collar on me. He pushed me down to my knees and I felt a dick being pressed against my lips. Whoever he was I started to suck him off. Then the blindfold was taken off me. It took a while for my eyes to adjust back to the light but I have to say that the guy fucking my mouth was HOT. He was real muscular, very built. He slid his cock out of my mouth and I didn't say a word as he led me to a low bench. He laid me on the bench face-up, securing each of my wrists to one of the legs of the bench. He also secured my ankles. The goddamned ball-stretcher was still around my balls. The muscle head attached a chain to the ball-stretcher and ran it under the bench, securing the other end to my slave collar. He pulled it tight so that if I moved my head I would pull meanly on my balls.

Then, he sauntered over to me and sat on my face, forcing me to rim him. DELICIOUS ass he had let me tell you. As I slurped away at it the photographer snapped picture after picture after picture. Then, the muscle dude turned around and again worked his hard dick into my mouth. I sucked him again...

After a while the hot top muscle guy left...

The photographer allowed me to put on a pair of shorts and a tank-top. We left his place and walked to the woods to continue the shoot.

This photo shoot lasted six hours and I have to say it was very hot...

ABOUT THE AUTHOR

Christopher Trevor

Christopher Trevor was born in July 1963 and grew up in New York City. As soon as he was old enough to know how he began writing fiction and has been writing gay erotic/fetish stories for the past ten to twelve years at this point. He became an avid reader as well from the time he knew how and reads everything from fiction, to non-fiction to biographies of interesting and unusual people, people who have made a difference or who have paved the way for others. Christopher attributes his writing artistic inspiration to artists such as Etienne, Tom of Finland, Tagame, The Hun, and most notably Joe T, who Christopher has had the pleasure of speaking with and even meeting over the last few years. Christopher states, "Joe T encouraged me to write about my fetish because I was embarrassed about it at the time. Joe T said that when we are embarrassed about something that makes it even more enticing somehow." Christopher totally agreed and never stopped writing in this genre. Erotic writers who inspired Christopher Trevor were: Tom Shaw (author of "That Day at the Quarry), C.S. White (author of Big Sur), Larry Townsend (author of countless erotic novels), and Mason Powell (author of the classic story "The Brig.")

Christopher discovered that not only did he enjoy writing erotic tales but that after his first bondage experience he had a genuine flair for it. Writing to erotic oriented magazines about his first bondage experience truly opened the floodgates for Christopher where this style of writing is concerned. Christopher thanks the handsome and muscular "Greg" for that experience way back in time. Christopher took "Creative Writing" courses every semester during his high school years and while other friends of his stopped writing what they loved to write about as time went on Christopher never let a day go by when he didn't write something... "I feel that if I don't write every day I will die," Christopher has said many times over.

Foot fetish stories and all things related; spanking fetish, erotic shaving, muscle bondage, tickle torture, and hardcore stories are just a few of the areas of gay eroticism that Christopher enjoys writing about and inspiring in others as well. As one internet buddy said to Christopher where the black socks fetish is concerned, "Until I started talking with you I never gave a thought to my socks when I got dressed for work in the morning. Now when I pull my dress socks on every morning I get a chill up my spine."

Christopher is proud of the erotic effect he has on people...

Christopher Trevor is also the author of:

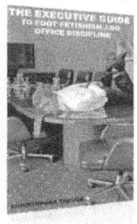 **The Executive Guide
to Foot Fetishism and
Office Discipline**

 **Timmy and
The Hong Kong Tailor**

 **Executive Ties That
Bind**

 **Love, Torture and
Redemption**

 **Don't! Stop! That
Tickles!**

 **Timmys Ticklish
Trials**

The Taming of Dominick

The Gym Instructor

Milked

The Military File

Erotic Street Blues

Quirks

The Abusive Wager

Timmy and the Evil Dr. Vonvellicator

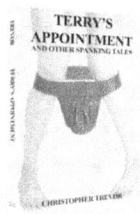

Terry's Appointment and Other Tickling Stories

Blackmail

Tickled Kink

Taking Liberties

Humiliation

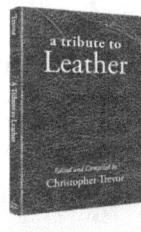

A Tribute to Leather

Discipline

Cleave and Otis

 *Revenge*

 *Men at Work*

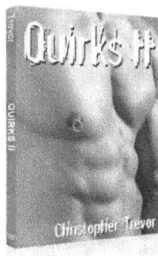 *Quirks II*

**Look for them where you bought this book,
Amazon.com or TheNazcaPlainsCorp.com.**